Hugo Hamilton was born in Dublin of Irish-German parentage. He has travelled extensively throughout Europe and brought elements of his dual identity to his novels *Surrogate City* and *The Last Shot*, which are also published by Faber and Faber in paperback. His work has appeared in other countries including Germany where his three novels have been set. His short fiction has appeared in the *Irish Times*, *New Irish Writing*, *Soho Square* and *First Fictions: Introduction 10*, and in his collection of stories *Dublin Where the Palm Tress Grow*. In 1992, he was awarded the Rooney Prize for Irish Literature. Hugo Hamilton lives and works in Dublin.

The Love Test

HUGO HAMILTON

faber and faber

LONDON · BOSTON

First published in 1995
by Faber and Faber Limited
3 Queen Square London WC1N 3AU
This paperback edition first published in 1996

Typeset by Wilmaset Ltd, Birkenhead, Wirral
Printed and bound in England by
Clays Ltd, St Ives plc

Hugo Hamilton is hereby identified as author of this work
in accordance with Section 77 of the Copyright,
Designs and Patents Act 1988.

A CIP record for this book is
available from the British Library

ISBN 0-571-17184-2

2 4 6 8 10 9 7 5 3 1

To the memory of
Walter Thräne
who died in Eisenhüttenstadt,
November 1993

Does this mean that, at a certain level of misfortune, love can no longer be generated?

Alexander Kluge

ONE

Claudia was being nice. She had prepared everything for dinner and brought out the special wine glasses. To finish off, it was damson tart. 'From the garden,' she boasted, cutting the triangular slices and placing them slowly on each plate, knowing that each movement was being watched. She was hoping to have brought back some of the tranquillity of their allotment garden on the edge of the city, with its wooden house, its fruitladen trees, the dreamy sound of bees or wasps, and the echoes from the lake. Perhaps it was possible to retrieve some of the memories, not just the distant images in family photo albums or on video reels but a real sense of being together again. As they ate the tart she talked of how she had been out to the allotment several times while Mathias was away, how she had cut the grass and watered everything, as though it was their marriage which had become parched during the summer and desperately needed water. And after dinner, in the living room, when Werner, their ten-year-old son, had gone back to his room to play computer games, she went around to the back of the sofa and embraced Mathias from behind. She said she was glad he was back and kissed the top of his head. Her hair fell down around his ears as she slid her hand into his shirt.

He was just back from a two-week seminar on political science in Salzburg. His mind was still fuelled by conference jokes and conference friendships. It was difficult to make the adjustment to home life, back in Berlin. The apartment looked smaller. The framed photograph he had once taken of Claudia in a forest still hung between the two windows, making her appear to him like somebody he knew a long time ago. Another memory of the three of them – mother, father and son chasing each other through the interconnecting rooms of their apartment – surfaced from even further back. Over dinner, as if to let him know how lonely she had been in his absence, Claudia said she had also read a lot, and she had found that every time the word 'shrug' came up she had involuntarily shrugged her shoulders. Werner had talked about leaving his football boots behind after practice, and Mathias asked if he had scored any goals, though he found he had hardly listened to his son. He wasn't really listening to Claudia either, and he had the feeling that even though she was now hugging him from behind, they were at opposite ends of a football stadium, calling to each other over the raucous crowds.

'Let's go out to the garden tomorrow,' Claudia suggested.

'I should go into the office,' he said, but she smiled and bit his ear, more like a warning he could not ignore.

Through the open windows of the courtyard they could hear television voices from other apartments, one close by, another further away. Claudia could make out the channel and the programme of the nearest one, a comedy which she might have watched herself. She was barefoot. For a moment she stood staring through the window as though she was still listening out for the jokes, trying to catch the humour. She put on some music and then left the room. Mathias closed his eyes. At Tegel airport, he had not seen her waiting for him in the crowd. No matter how often he had come back from assignments like this, it felt more than ever like walking on to a stage. She had to wave at him as though he were blind and their embrace in the arrival lounge seemed unreal somehow, or so familiar perhaps as to turn them into complete strangers again. It was not until later, when he heard her sneeze twice in quick succession in the kitchen, that he had any sense of being at home. He could not tell how long he had felt this paralysis, except that Claudia had initiated discussions from time to time about the lack of warmth in their

2

marriage; they used positive terms like rejuvenation, openness, love – words which seemed to sound a note of alarm. After ten years of marriage, it was not easy to regain the momentum of earlier years.

The brash, high-pitched sound of Turkish music suddenly came in from across the courtyard to compete with Tom Waits. Now he knew he was home. It jolted him back to old grievances; he had the instant urge to complain but instead tolerated the collision of cultures until Claudia came back and closed the windows. The light had begun to fade outside.

'Shall I do your feet?' she suggested, setting up a footstool beside him.

'Not now, Claudia. Please.'

He opened his eyes and saw that she was looking at him. Up to then, his gaze must have fallen short of her eyes. He thought he perceived something vulnerable about her and submitted. She had taken an interest in reflexology, a small attempt to change her life, a new challenge which really turned out to be quite unfulfilling and would never replace the longing for something more radically different. She was looking for renewal in her heart. He recalled some of their arguments in the past, how she had accused him of being conventional, and how he had condescended, laughing at the notion of reflexology making a difference to cancer patients. Mathias obediently placed his feet on the footstool and allowed Claudia to remove his shoes and socks. The shock of air hit the soles of his feet and the spaces between the toes.

It struck her that he had not asked her anything about herself, nothing personal. Perhaps she had volunteered too easily. So much of what they said to each other from day to day was administrative. And there was so much they knew about each other that, at times, it seemed to make real communication impossible. Whenever they laughed together at something, it was usually because of Werner: something on TV, or with friends; something extraneous. It struck her how solitary two

3

people could be together, more so perhaps than people living on their own. It was his fault, after all, that the spell had been broken. Three years ago, around Werner's seventh birthday, she had discovered that Mathias had been unfaithful during one of his trips abroad. It was not something you could forget. It had left a scar, an underlying sense of mistrust resurfacing like malaria at the oddest times.

The smell of oils had been unleashed from their bottles. Mathias felt the warmth of her hands as she lifted his feet to place a towel underneath. It offered reassurance and trust and simultaneously proved how vulnerable feet were.

'Relax,' she commanded, kneading from the soles up to the toes in firm strokes.

But there was an unconcealed resistance, as though he were close to breaking into laughter all the time. She felt the tension again and again, and eventually demanded his co-operation.

'Come on, Matt,' she pleaded. He made a renewed effort. For a while, she worked confidently, but the underlying tension in his body never submitted to this massage and she suddenly sighed and leaned forward, still holding on to his delicate feet.

'Look, Matt, have you got something to tell me?'

She might as well have driven a thumbnail into his heel. Pinned between impulsive denial and incomprehension, he did not know quite how to answer. This kind of reckoning never came until later, when they were in bed, before lovemaking, or during, or just after.

'What do you mean?' he said. His eyes gave off the appearance of instant hurt. 'Claudia, come on.'

'You're so tense, Matt. I know there's something. I can feel it.'

Mathias sat up. He didn't want to be drawn into some new offensive, or to reopen old ones. He smiled at her, not like the casual smiles they had exchanged at the airport or in the car on the way home, but a deliberate smile which now made him appear even more distant. She asked him was he not glad to be back home. He could have stayed away longer. She made it seem as though there were some oath of family allegiance he had broken. Her voice had become tough and her eyes had withdrawn their warmth.

'Look, Claudia, I don't know what you're getting at. I'm just back home two hours and you start accusing me.'

'I'm not accusing you,' she said. 'I never ask what you do when you're away. Never. All I'm asking you is to be honest. I'm honest with you, am I not?'

He forced a laugh. 'Just because I'm a little tense maybe . . .'

All the old reassurances had to be given, as though ten years of their lives spent together meant nothing at that moment, as though he had to go back to the beginning in order to reassert his allegiance all over again, fighting his way back up like in a game of snakes and ladders. She let go of his feet.

'I just don't know what you're worried about, Claudia.'

Mathias wished there was something really original he could say, something that would help him ascend quickly and make him less of an outsider. She ended her massage abruptly, began to pack away the oils again and stood up. Then it crossed his mind that her accusations made her look guilty. What was on her mind that made her so suspicious of him?

'Claudia,' he said. 'Are you finished with my feet?'

She ignored the jibe, just picked up her bag of oils and left.

'And wipe your feet,' she said. 'I don't want that oil dragged all over the carpet.'

She had placed him back in the position of having to come and get her. After a short intermission he would have to follow her into the bedroom and slowly regain her trust, choosing the right words, incrementally building up understanding, bit by bit. At the right moment, and he was such a good judge of that precise moment, he would make an outright denial, or declaration of love. After an initial kiss, he would then extract an equal declaration from her, reclaiming the baseline of their affections. He would stroke her hair, or her hand, and slowly, perhaps even hours later, his body would take over from the words. But

5

would that be enough? Would it bring them together again like lovers?

Mathias wiped his feet with the towel and stood up. He went over to the first window and opened it again. The courtyard was dark now, and he could see right into the apartments on the other side. Some rooms were lit up like aquariums from the TV. The people in the Turkish apartment had closed their windows and he could see children dancing with old people. Above them, Mathias watched a couple washing up together after dinner. In another apartment at the same level there was a young woman getting dressed, standing in her bra, trying on different jackets, while up higher a man was working on some kind of sculpture that looked like a giant egg cup.

After ten minutes Mathias went in to Werner and talked to him. They played a short game of computer golf which his son won. He lightly slapped the back of Werner's head and told him not to stay up all night, turning around again from the door to say goodnight and to look around at the chaos which reigned in the boy's room. In the kitchen Mathias poached another thin slice of damson tart and then began to take the plates out of the dishwasher and stack them; each sound went out through the apartment like an advance message to Claudia. He took two beers from the fridge and joined her in the bedroom.

TWO

Claudia had just come back from the lake and her hair was wet, clinging to her skull like a tight bathing cap. The gate made a tiny squeak, and she stood on the garden path in her blue and white swimwear, still a little out of breath from the swim.

'Absolutely gorgeous,' she announced.

Mathias and Werner looked around when she spoke. They were standing under the trees, picking up the plums which had fallen in the past few days. They had two buckets, one for rejects and one for the good crop which would go into future damson tarts to be made by Claudia's mother. Now and again they ate a damson, feeling for softness first, biting into it, then examining the green-brown flesh of the remaining part and casting away the stone. Wasps had discovered the buckets. The grass under the trees had hardly grown at all that summer; all over it was yellow and tough like straw, leaving bald patches of hard, dry soil.

'Werner, I hope you wash them before you eat them,' Claudia said.

'Try one, Mama,' Werner said.

But Claudia shook her head. The sweet smoke from the barbecue coals was already beginning to fill the air with the promise of food. Beyond their garden, a lawnmower hummed in the distance like the sound of bees. In the neighbouring allotments people were weeding flowerbeds, repairing fences or fussing over barbecues of their own against the background babble of shrieking voices from the lake shore. A lawn sprinkler nearby kept up a faint, rhythmic sneezing, while in the sky over

7

the lake a light aircraft pulled a message through the air, too far away to be recognized. It all reinforced the calm security of this lakeside allotment outside Berlin; a continuous silence punctuated by the perpetual inventory of tiny leisure sounds: laughter, ice in drinks, music in the open air and the occasional rush of bicycle tires grinding along the sandy lane down towards the shore. The familiarity of all this harboured so many recollections of good times for Claudia that it sometimes showed up the lacklustre present. At certain brief moments the tranquillity tipped over into a sense of suffocation, as though this family sanctuary, away from work, away from all danger and reality, was so bound up with overwhelming intimacies that it occasionally represented a kind of family cage.

She smiled at Mathias and Werner without thinking, the way she sometimes drove through the city without being aware of driving. Inside the wooden house, she went upstairs and took a shower. It gave her a subconscious sense of pride to see in the mirror that her body was evenly tanned. She looked well. Or was it some feeling of desire she felt, some indiscriminate hunger for adventure? She had long ago rejected any notion of avenging Mathias's infidelities and wondered what suddenly provoked this new impulse to get away; was it a kind of marriage-panic, a longing for society, for fun, something new? In a flash, this surge of illogical desire went away again and she submitted once more to the passive numbness of the garden house.

She and Mathias had bought the allotment together before they were married, before Werner was born; some time after their trip to Ireland. It had always remained in their minds as an extract from that holiday, a piece of the west of Ireland to which they could flee every weekend. As she got dressed again she recalled how the garden house looked when they bought it first, a simple, no water or electricity dream which they went on improving from year to year until, in a way, its very perfection now endangered everything. If their marriage was undergoing a

8

sort of unspoken trial right now, it was because Claudia felt she wanted more of that original simplicity.

She decided to wear shorts and T-shirt, and a thin layer of lipstick. She called Werner inside and helped him get his gear ready to meet his friends after lunch. She fussed over him, asking what shorts he was going to wear, worrying that he was a bit too young for power boats and skiing. Sometimes she feared that all her hopes had been transferred to her son. She wondered if Werner had already started thinking about girls. It would happen soon, as suddenly as he had become interested in all that techno music, for instance.

Mathias had already begun to cook the food, talking to himself or to anyone who might listen to him expatiating on the principles of barbecuing; when to turn over the meat, how to avoid the fat bursting into flames and charring the food. Claudia encouraged him in the hope that he would always hold on to his unequalled expertise at outdoor cooking. She prepared the salad and began talking about the homegrown tomatoes she had received that morning from one of the neighbours.

Over lunch, the subject of tomatoes developed into a fullscale lecture from Mathias on the ecology and the latest attempt to clone a new long-lasting tomato. Claudia and Werner exchanged glances and smiled at each other.

'I think your father is having another thought,' she said, but Mathias ignored her and went on talking. Even if Claudia occasionally admired his knowledge, she was concerned about his obsessions with facts. He was in danger of becoming a walking encyclopedia rather than a husband or a father. She forked up a slice of tomato from the salad bowl and held it up a little menacingly towards Mathias.

'You can't get better than that,' she announced, before throwing the exhibit into her mouth, humming as the taste of homegrown tomato and basil exploded on her palate. 'Mmmmm,' she moaned. 'I can tell you right now, if I had been in the Garden of Eden, it would have been a tomato.'

What was she getting at, Mathias asked himself. He searched her eyes but she smiled back, putting her hand on his arm.

After lunch, Werner disappeared, followed by a trail of endearments and shouts of caution. With the long Saturday afternoon ahead of them, Mathias would like to have stayed at the garden reading or simply relaxing in each other's presence, with no need to talk much, only to exist on the edge of an indolent trance in the afternoon heat. But Claudia had other plans. She wanted action. Having phoned their close friends Alexandra and Klaus earlier on, she had already promised to join them on the beach near their allotment, some ten minutes away in the car. Klaus and Alexandra had invited lots of people: Dieter and Stefan, their gay friends, and Kevin, the Irishman.

'Klaus is going to give you windsurfing lessons,' she said with great enthusiasm.

'You must be joking,' Mathias said, but Claudia embraced him and laughed affectionately, rubbing her hand along his back and buttocks, finally trying to persuade him to come with a series of baby sounds and gentle slaps.

'It'll be fun, Matt.'

'I don't like their beach any more,' Mathias said, attempting a token resistance. He was all for nature, but had somehow come to prefer the regular beach and the privacy of clothes, however scant. The sight of nude colonies stretched out along the shore near Klaus and Alexandra's allotment always made him uneasy. There was the usual gay posturing of Dieter and Stefan, Alexandra's new tattoo at the top of her right thigh and all the initial self-conscious comparisons on a nudist beach. It was disturbing to be faced with a whole spectrum of genitalia, from four to seventy-four, parading up and down the shale in trainers; the forlorn, leering old men in sunglasses staring up everybody's asshole, or the knockout shape of an eighteen-year-old girl who insisted on playing volley ball or frisbee with her Adonis boyfriend close by.

Mathias remained silent, agreeing to go by default. He was

momentarily caught up with the Garden of Eden and the idea that marriage forced them to hide from each other behind the privacy of clothes. He and Claudia had been driven out of paradise into a world of tact and caution. At home there was a new code of privacy; she no longer allowed him to walk into the bathroom while she was having a bath, he dressed quickly so as to prevent any hint of a paunch, and the lighting in the bedroom had taken on more subtlety. All these precautions in order to keep their distance. Would they ever get back to the time when they trusted each other completely?

Alexandra greeted Mathias and Claudia with beer and kisses. She was still dressed. The others had already gone down to the beach, and Mathias followed them immediately while Claudia spent some time sitting under a vine-clad awning talking to Alexandra. She was aware that Alexandra had met Mathias before she did, long ago, when they were all at university together. Occasionally she wondered if Mathias still attributed any significance to it, whether it was a good memory or an empty one. Any possibility of his going back to Alexandra had subsided over the years, even if the risk had never completely gone away. Drinking coffee from chipped *Jurassic Park* mugs, they talked about children, how Alexandra wanted a baby but Klaus was against it.

'It's either that or an affair,' Alexandra joked, and it seemed as though these were suddenly the only options a woman had.

Later, when they joined the others on the beach, Mathias and Klaus were already standing on the shore assembling the windsurfing gear. Stefan's high-pitched laugher could be heard 200 metres away, and Claudia instantly recalled the night Stefan made a play for her, just when all the straight couples thought he was safe. For weeks after that she had become fascinated by what gay men got up to at night.

The Country and Western fanatics from one of the allotments nearby were all gathered around a large barbecue further up the shore, close to a wigwam. How Country and Western could you

11

be on a nudist beach? One woman made the concession of wearing a stetson while another wore nothing but a Davy Crockett trapper's hat. Klaus and Alexandra had once been invited over by the Country and Western neighbours and found them all talking English among themselves in a Texan drawl. Even when they made the leap back to German out of necessity, they kept up the Country twang.

Claudia and Alexandra took off their clothes. There was nothing strange about this, not even at that moment of sudden nudity. The star-shaped tattoo on Alexandra's thigh looked smaller this time. Claudia wondered if she should remove her earrings, and if lipstick wasn't a form of apparel too? She shook hands with all of the others and sat down. Kevin, the man from Ireland, was white as marble except for the redness around the nose and shoulders where the sun was beginning to bite. Alexandra persuaded him to accept her factor eight while Stefan began to translate a joke for his benefit.

Claudia watched Mathias's attempt to take off on the lake before he promptly fell in and the brightly coloured sail flapped down on to the surface of the water like a large butterfly wing. She laughed out loud, as if to demonstrate her own misgivings about Mathias. Wearing nothing but a baseball cap, Klaus went in to his waist, laughing and splashing his palms downwards in defeat at his protégé's failure. The sun left a bright metallic sheen across the lake and from time to time a plane overhead silenced everything. Silhouettes of more capable windsurfers sailed about at speed against the glare, legs apart, backside to the wind. Beyond them in the distance there were people water-skiing and, further still, tilted yachts in full sail.

There was something strange, something tragic perhaps, about seeing Mathias's figure standing on water for an instant, Claudia thought. She would laugh at this again later when they were in bed together. She would stab him in the ribs with her finger and poke fun at his failure. She had never been attracted to windsurfing. Even with clothes on, the sport seemed to lack a certain fundamental aesthetic. But without clothes, any integrity it might have had was lost, and the figures became virtually obscene. For Mathias's first brief moment afloat, his body struck a series of disturbing poses; crouching, sticking his bottom out for ballast, then jerking up straight and thrusting his hips forward before collapsing backwards into the water.

THREE

On Sunday morning Claudia lay in bed talking to Werner. The room still smelled of coffee and an empty cup stood on each of the bedside cupboards. Mathias had gone into the kitchen to finish off the report on his conference in Salzburg, leaving Claudia behind alone with Werner.

Werner had taken a jar of small coins down from the dressing table and, after trying to count them first, began idly placing them in rows along the bedcover. Every time she moved to stretch herself it would disturb the lines and he would tell her to remain still. They were talking about the future; she had asked him what he wanted to be when he grew up, and they got into a long rambling discussion about strange careers. Claudia was better at this kind of talk than her husband. He tended to lecture too much. She liked to ask questions and hear Werner speak for himself.

After a little reflection, Werner thought he wanted to be a pilot, or an archaeologist most of all. Claudia asked him why he had changed his mind from the last time when he wanted to become a palaeontologist, but Werner said he wanted to be that too. She didn't try to influence him the way Mathias might have done. She preferred to give in to the fantasy of a child, making time stand still. These were the kind of long aimless conversations she used to have with Mathias in the early days, before his work made everything else seem so trivial. She longed for that timeless aftermath of love, a drowsy cosiness on the edge of Sunday morning boredom where nothing mattered.

By now, Werner had turned her into a corpse with his coins. Her arms, outside the duvet, were lined with chains of 50 pfennig pieces so that she was no longer able move them. All she could do was speak, and she asked Werner if being a pilot would be very satisfying.

'Would it not be a bit boring doing the same thing all the time?'

'No,' Werner answered. 'Don't you do the same things all the time?'

'I don't think so,' she said, though she knew it was a lie. The conversation had suddenly touched on reality. She longed to do something very different in her life. 'I never do the same thing twice,' she said.

'Yes you do. What about getting dressed? That's the same thing.'

'No it isn't,' she said, smiling. 'It's a new experience every time. It might as well have never happened to me before.'

'That's stupid, Mama. You drive the car again and again.'

'Ah yes, but each time it's new. Everything I do is for the first time. And the next time I do it, it's completely new to me.'

Werner realized that she was joking. Claudia knew she was lying to herself as well. Perhaps it was touching on the frail reality of her life, like a sensitive tooth. The accidental veracity of this lazy discussion with Werner brought a mild emotional panic to her thoughts. She laughed, causing some of the coins to fall off her arms. He told her to be still while he replaced them. And as the conversation proceeded, he began to place coins on her face, starting with her cheeks and her chin, then erecting towers of coins on her forehead so that she could hardly move at all any more. She was being confined by these metaphysical weights pressing down on her personality, like a female Gulliver pinned down by her own family. Only the calm, humorous sound of Werner's voice stopped her from struggling free and running out of the room, away to a place where she could be alone, an individual.

'You go to the toilet,' Werner said.

'Trust you to say that,' she retorted, but then one of the columns collapsed and the cool coins slipped down into the bed around her neck and shoulders.

Werner erected a new pillar in its place, along with a low column of coins on her upper lip which soon prevented her from saying any more that the word 'never' in defiance. She was being silenced in this debate. Her eyes were closed over with larger coins, and while Werner kept announcing things she had repeated in her life, Claudia had become mummified in money.

After lunch they all drove over to Claudia's mother together, something they repeated religiously every fortnight. There was a new friction between Claudia and Mathias, but they agreed to silence during the visit. Mathias parked the car and Werner carried the plastic damson pail covered with a gingham tea towel. The boy was instantly showered with kisses as his grandmother took the bucket from him and led him into the kitchen to show him the newly baked chocolate horeshoes. The old labrador ran around in excitement, shaking his tail.

'And for the adults,' Claudia's mother announced, lifting the paper cover momentarily for a sneak preview of the fresh damson tart. Mathias made a face towards Werner while Claudia's mother had her back turned. Claudia slapped his arm.

Every Sunday they alternated the afternoon coffee and cake between Mathias's parents and Claudia's mother. Claudia's father had left ten years ago, after thirty years of marriage. He had left shortly after advising Claudia and Mathias on the renovations to their garden house. As a timber consultant he found it easy to leave suddenly, moving down to the south of Germany, near Freiburg. He had a new woman in his life now. Claudia still met him once a year when he came back to Berlin, but it all left its mark on the notion of stability, as though he were some kind of pioneer of separation, forcing everyone else to re-evaluate their own sense of freedom whenever they remembered him. He could take no more of the damson tart, Mathias had once remarked. Watching Frau Beniers hurrying around the kitchen, he could see that she still had that forsaken look, the underlying admission that her life was a failure. Claudia, her daughter, could never shake off the hereditary omen foreshadowing the inevitable review of her own situation. Each divorce in Germany seemed to hang like a cloud over intact marriages, like a provocation or a dare, forcing every other partnership to measure its own durability against all odds. The casualties infecting the healthy.

But Claudia had a robust attitude. She still liked to believe that her life with Mathias was unique. 'For ever' was an expression to be avoided. So too was the intellectual cynicism that grew out of boredom. It was important to prevent the marriage from becoming a form of imprisonment, people sharing the same cell for life together, undergoing this constant test of over-exposure. She stressed the positive angles, the fact that she still belonged to society – work, friends, cinema, parties, holidays; even shopping, or driving through the streets of Berlin, or the occasional need to vote in elections added up collectively to a free life. But the absence of fun and passion sometimes reduced these freedoms to nothing. And according to the statistics, marriage in Germany was only meant to last while it was fun. Her partnership with Mathias occasionally appeared to clog up or congeal, like a stifling institution made sacred by their son and the weekly visits to grandparents. The satisfaction of lineage. The refuge of cosy banalities.

Claudia's mother brought in the coffee. Werner underwent a brief interrogation before he could pick up his glass of Coke and a horseshoe biscuit. When he was younger he used to ask to stay behind with his grandparents. Now he was waiting for the adult talk to take over so that he could start reading the comics he had brought with him.

Claudia had practical matters to discuss. Her mother's forthcoming trip to Hanover to stay with relatives had to be planned out in advance; train timetables, taxis, and who would look after the dog. Even though her mother had made the journey many times before, Claudia insisted on forecasting each cup of coffee and sandwich break along the route in advance. Otherwise her mother might change her mind and stay at home.

Werner was petting the labrador with one hand, a comic in the other. Claudia wore a loose, patterned red skirt. Occasionally when she shifted in her seat she allowed Mathias, sitting opposite her, to look at her legs. It made her think of him as a complete stranger. She still had an obligation to attract strangers.

The empty plates on the table were stained pink with the mixture of damson dye and cream. Claudia's mother had misgivings about kennels; Mathias tried to set her mind at rest.

Out of mischief, Claudia tried to make eye contact with him, trying to generate a private moment of intimacy between them; some secret sign of affection while Werner was preoccupied with his comics and Claudia's mother had begun to tidy up.

'Frau Beniers, you have absolutely nothing to worry about,' Mathias repeated.

He seemed to be ignoring the attempt at intimacy. Claudia tried it again, this time blowing him a kiss and smiling as though a moment of lovers' anarchy, while her mother's back was turned, could underline how close she and Mathias had always been. The frivolity of this action gave Claudia a thrill and reminded her of the way things were in the beginning. But Mathias misread it completely and, suspecting that she was making fun of his earnest manner, began to glare back at her. Her expression of affection failed and snapped over into indifference instead. When the old labrador came around to her side of the sofa, Claudia dropped her plot and examined the dog's paws.

'My God, Mama, we need to get his nails done again.'

Claudia undertook to have him checked over by the vet, and when the dog turned away she began to examine him from behind.

'Mathias, what do you think? Does he need to have his glands squeezed again?'

'Sure, get them squeezed,' Mathias replied with thinly veiled sarcasm. His face bore the rictus of bitterness and boredom.

FOUR

Mathias was in his office at the *Tageszeitung* on Tuesday afternoon. He had already put the toughest, first day back at work behind him, reintegrating fast and getting down to new projects with regenerated vigour. His appetite for success as a journalist had put his own private life into the background again. That afternoon he was waiting to speak to a woman whom he had agreed to help as a favour to some friends in Bundnis 90, the East German self-awareness group. But in the meantime, Claudia was on the phone, still asking him to see about her mother's dog.

'Claudia, I can't do it,' he said impatiently. 'I'm up to my eyes.'

'Matt, come on, I can't get out of work. You know where the kennels are. I'll take Mama to the train.'

It irritated Mathias that Claudia still thought he could simply drop things and look after domestic matters at any time of the day. To Claudia, his reluctance appeared like disloyalty, or a sign that other things mattered more than his family. In the early days of their marriage he had always been able to free himself at a moment's notice to meet her for lunch, even to stop by at home with her. Now he had a career to think of. Two of his *Tageszeitung* colleagues had recently moved on, one to the *Spiegel*, one to the ZDF.

An East German woman in her late thirties was shown into his office. He pointed to a chair and she sat down, looking around, fanning herself a little as if she had brought the dry, stagnant heat of the afternoon in with her from the street. The distant sounds of traffic came through the open windows. Beyond the glass partition of the office, a journalist next door worked in apparent silence against the background of desks, computer terminals and the general chaos of the newspaper office; an atmosphere of sloth and panic all at once.

'Claudia, I've got to go.'

Mathias gave her thirty seconds more while he made an assessment of the woman in his office. Not bad at all, he reckoned, even though she was about ten years older than he was. Wonderful legs, he thought, making an habitual, sub-conscious comparison with Claudia's legs. He hastily ended the conversation with his wife, stood up and proffered his hand to the East German woman.

'Mathias Hauser,' he said. 'They told me about you. Christa Süsskind? Wasn't there something about forced adoption?'

'Yes,' the woman answered, then hesitated.

Mathias encouraged her with a look of professional sincerity, but she stared back into his eyes as though unable to say much more, other than awkwardly blurting out what was most prominent in her mind.

'They took my baby,' she said.

Mathias tried to make it easier for her to talk and go through the facts slowly. She told him she had been in Hohenschönhausen prison. He patiently made notes, interjecting every now and again to encourage her or to ask specific questions. He wanted to know the date of birth of the baby. In order to put her at her ease, he also asked her more conversational questions, like where she was living and where she was employed. She was a former nurse from Leipzig, now working for a dentist in Berlin.

Mathias wondered if there was anything at all he could do for her. He had generally allied himself to the cause of women, but these East German stories had been through the papers already.

'Who was in charge of Hohenschönhausen?' he asked, digging for something new.

'Erwin Pückler,' she answered, and he could see the first sign of hate crossing her face.

21

'Yes, I've heard of him,' Mathias said.

'He was such a *Schweinhund*,' she said, narrowing her eyes. 'If you'll pardon me, Herr Hauser.'

Mathias noted the slightly archaic, East German use of '*Schweinhund*'. He allowed her to elaborate, but though she hinted at the horrors of Hohenschönhausen prison she soon became reticent. It was as though she had a feeling that past injustices in the East were not relevant any more.

'The problem is that Pückler is missing,' Mathias said. 'Underground.'

He knew of half a dozen journalists actively hunting for Erwin Pückler, one of the truly original GDR ghouls, who had left a trail of human wreckage up to the fall of the Wall. Catching up with him would be a real scoop, but he still wasn't sure if he should get involved. He considered the task of finding this woman's baby. He stared at her bare arms, and once again stopped himself searching for the imprint of a bra strap. He left the office for a moment and came back with coffee. She thanked him as he placed the cup on the desk beside her, clearing a deluge of papers and magazines away with his elbow. In the process he knocked over an old cup, spilling a thick brown tongue of liquid over the desk, just missing an open judicial reference book. He wiped it quickly with printout paper which he threw into an overfilled basket. He offered her a small pink ice-cream scoop as a substitute spoon.

'We got a big bag of them from the ice-cream place around the corner,' he said, watching for the smile on her face. But then he had the impression that his easygoing West German style lacked an appropriate seriousness. He made some further notes, allowing her to examine the few grey hairs around his temples in order to gain her trust. Instead she stared at his clothes, finally concentrating on his shoes as though East Germans could tell a person's character by their footwear.

'OK,' Mathisa said. 'What I suggest is this. We go out to Hohenschönhausen together and get some pictures of you. I'll arrange everything. Then we run a picture with a small story, just to get people thinking.'

'I don't want my whole life story published.'

Mathias was taken aback. The hate which she had shown towards the past seemed like nothing to the hostility and opposition she expressed towards the dominant West. She said she didn't come here to be used or sucked up by a Wessie newspaper. She paused a moment to stare at him, as though he'd said something obscene. It seemed his proposal had become an example of the running arrogance displayed by Westerners towards former East Germans. Mathias watched her getting all worked up, voicing a bitter disappointment which appeared to echo that of her subsumed nation. She had been under the impression that he was going to help her.

'Now hold on one minute, Fräulein Süsskind,' Mathias said, showing a little impatience. 'I know this is tough, you've been through hard times, but you tell me, why did you come all the way to this office on a hot day like this if you didn't want to tell us what happened?'

She hesitated again, shrinking back at the sound of authority. He must have appeared like a Stasi, perhaps, interrogating her.

'I just want to find my baby,' she said, almost on the brink of tears.

'I understand. But this is the only chance you've got, Fräulein Süsskind,' he said. 'People are known to read the *Tageszeitung*, you know. Somebody might contact us with some information.'

He smiled at her, a gesture which helped to diffuse the confrontation. Beyond the glass partition, one of the journalists was imperviously applying eye-liner. A pigeon flew past the window casting a flash shadow. In trying to persuade her, Mathias realized that he had involuntarily promised to help. She began to examine his shoes once more.

FIVE

The whole thing started back in Leipzig, in the days of the GDR, when Christa Süsskind had an affair with a married man, much older than her. She was only twenty at the time. Ralf Krone was just short of twice her age, a professor of chemical engineering at the Karl Marx University in Leipzig. But he was handsome and courteous, qualities she found lacking in men of her own age. He generated excitement. He could make her laugh, though at the risk of being a little crude and politically indiscreet, a matter which soon brought their affair to the attention of the state. Neighbours, university colleagues, porters, café staff and general observers began to talk, and when they had known each other scarcely two months the Stasi closed in.

Christa and Ralf were both drunk one night and arrived home, climbing up the stairs to her apartment, giggling. She could hardly get the key into the door. He was biting at her shoulder, and once they were inside she remarked, looking down into the street through the window, on the way he had parked the car. His driving was reckless. Then he demanded more cognac and wanted to dance around the apartment. When she asked him more about his work at the university, he told her he examined the reproductive drive of mice and compared it statistically to the people in communist societies. When he was drunk, he sometimes became seditious.

'I'm serious – Honecker wants everyone to fuck like mice,' he said.

She switched on the radio and agreed to dance with him

instead. She had no idea that she was being watched, no more than did anyone else in the GDR who was being watched in those days. But even if she had suspected that the MfS had placed a bug in her apartment it might have made no difference, because there was something about love and pleasure in the East German state which had become purely subversive. Pleasure was freedom. Perhaps there were certain things she might have whispered, or concealed, or left unsaid altogether, but there was little fear in her life because the affair seemed to exist on another plane, far from the banal and empty grey background of life in Leipzig at the time.

At the Stasi offices in Runde Ecke, the state held its constant vigil, observing the progress of pleasure as much as any liberal, anti-state smalltalk. In a small office surrounded by recording equipment, wire leads and maps of Leipzig, four Stasi men listened to Christa Süsskind and Ralf Krone consummate their affair. Sandwiches with semicircles of wurst peering out from between the bread lay on a table. The men's hats were discarded in various places around the room and the acoustic facia board behind them held lists of names and telephone numbers. On another wall hung faded nude posters, yellowing with age, evoking only a dull, exhausted sexual inspiration. The intention of the state appeared to be some general attempt to reduce all love affairs to the same lacklustre images of old pin-ups.

'It's Krone all right,' one of the men confirmed.

They telephoned upstairs and were joined by a senior officer. The listening room came to attention. The men became instantly aware of their rank in the same way that, at a moment's notice, each man could recognize his own hat. They waited a while for more proof, listening to the couple talking and laughing. One of the officers was blowing his nose. It had become clear that the couple were dancing because, in the next moment, there was a crashing sound over the speakers as Christa and Ralf collided with the furniture, rocking the table and chairs.

'Really, Ralf, your dancing is as bad as your driving,' she said.

One of the officers kept making notes. Others made some lewd comments and lit cigarettes, filling the recording room with blue smoke. Then there was a prolonged silence and the men waited in shocked attention, following every sound in the vivid progression of love as though they were taking part themselves. Even the tired nudes on the walls seemed to take on new meaning.

'Come here, my little mouse,' Ralf Krone was heard saying.

'No, Ralf.'

'Mousey! Mousey! Mousey!'

The intervals of deep silence began to increase. Every now and then they were punctuated by a series of intimate endearments, which were potentially embarrassing to the men listening in. One of the officers briefly simulated copulation with a swivel chair and stopped again as the others laughed dutifully, or self-consciously; the mere suggestion of sex acting on them like blind terror. It forced everyone to re-evaluate their own sexual abilities; brought back all the irrational, youthful anxieties over size and performance and made them feel like they were lagging behind in a contest among males. It produced feelings of jealousy and bitterness, rage, even a brief impulse to murder; as if each of them were being forced to observe the infidelity of their own wife or partner. Self-esteem was restored only by their roles as policemen upholding state authority. The officer in charge smiled with satisfaction and asked once again if they were certain it was Ralf Krone. And as it became clear that Christa had begun to remove her clothes, the atmosphere in the listening room became triumphant.

'Bravo, Herr Krone,' the senior officer said, and then left the room again.

The remaining officers went on listening, each fitting up his own visual parade of images, each imagining the apartment and the furniture and every interior detail surrounding this couple. When one of the officers sneezed and began to blow his nose again, the rest of the men glared at him. The couple over the speakers had begun to talk again. She was saying something.

'Ralf, I love you, but aren't you going to take your socks off?'

When the Stasi men came to pick up Ralf Krone at the university, he was still so overwhelmed by the previous night with Christa that he failed to grasp the reality of his situation. As they drove him away under the gaze of his students and out through the stagnant, polluted streets of Leipzig, his mind was still inflamed with images of recent sex. A strong consciousness of his own body had been restored by contact with hers.

It was only when the unmarked Stasi car stopped outside a small, old-fashioned café that he felt the old instinctive fear of authority. With it came the dull recognition of failure in his marriage, throbbing like the after-effects of alcohol under his skull. Inadvertently, it was his wife who had caused all the trouble with State Security when she began to nurture a desperate desire to go abroad. Having seen pictures of rugged coastal countries like Scotland and Ireland, they had found the love in their marriage replaced by this impossible longing for the sea. Ralf tried everything at first, applying for exit visas, bringing upon himself all the attention of the MfS, who wanted to know why a chemical engineer expressed such an interest in leaving their perfect little Soviet state. When Ralf eventually dropped his application, he was suddenly elevated to the rank of professor. Then, six months later, the Stasi had come looking for him again as a recruit. He had put them off.

This time he knew what to expect; it was an old tune and he realized he had been brought to a Stasi café. Two men sat waiting for him. Oak panels separated sections of the café for privacy.

Above the coat stand hung the usual sign disclaiming responsibility for the '*garderobe*', and Ralf recalled the joke Christa made about restaurants bearing no responsibility for what people wore. The proprietress wore grey stockings. She had too much rouge on her cheeks and the wide circumference of her hair gave the impression she had been mildly electrocuted, an overall apearance which seemed to show deliberate contempt for the beauty techniques of the West. Obviously on the Stasi payroll, Ralf thought. Her husband was slowly pulling golden, frothy tulips of beer, and under his feet the lino had been worn through to the wood.

The two officers introduced themselves and quickly brought up the subject of Ralf's recruitment. One of them, named Stanjek, had come all the way from Berlin to offer him a new post in the science division of the MfS. When Ralf instinctively turned down the offer, the officer from Berlin seemed dumbfounded and continued to present the post as a once in a lifetime opportunity.

Beer arrived at the table. The officers toasted his health. Ralf thanked them for the beer, but said he wasn't accepting the job. He reminded them that he had refused the post before, and it was only after some persistence that the men seemed to realize they had come up against untypical GDR stubbornness. They exchanged looks, a signal that seemed to declare a state monopoly on tenacity. The Berlin officer allowed his colleague to take over.

'Herr Krone, I believe you have a problem with your socks,' the local Leipzig officer said.

'What are you getting at?' Ralf asked. Was this some Stasi attempt at humour?

Showing no signs of hurry, the second officer began to place his briefcase on his knees, then took out a transcript and began to read from it, placing a cassette tape on the table in front of Ralf in the same moment. The words were instantly familiar.

'Honecker wants everyone to fuck like mice . . .' the officer whispered. 'Am I right?'

They had recorded everything. Feverishly, Ralf scanned back over the last night with Christa. Huge gaps seemed to have appeared in his memory.

'Mousey, Mousey, Mousey . . .'

What had they said to each other? For a split second, Ralf began to suspect her of arranging this. Was Christa on the payroll too? He thought back to see if he could discover where he had been conned.

He and Christa had struck up a tacit pact of such openness and trust that he could hardly conceive betrayal. They had met at the Leipzig fair that spring and got talking while she was helping a friend out on a ceramics exhibit. They seemed to be at once in the same frame of mind, somewhere outside society, belonging to some lighthearted race. With Christa, he abandoned all the habitual safeguards of communist society. She inspired none of the dishonesty which dogged him when he went after other women. She simply assumed he was married. The Leipzig fair of lost husbands, she called it.

She expected him to lie. He even had trouble initially convincing her that he was a professor of chemical engineering. At first she had let on she was a schoolteacher, then a librarian, only confiding that she was a nurse once he had asked her out to dinner. And over dinner she told him it was all right with her if he wasn't a chemical engineer either.

The second officer spoke again, putting the state ultimatum to him. They knew he had been carrying on with 'Blondi', as they called her. Either he would accept the post in Berlin, or he would be disgraced and lose his position at the university.

'You'll be working in the sewers, my friend. And you'll have more than smelly socks.'

'I'm not taking this job,' Ralf said once more, shaking his head. The heat generated by the alcohol began to rush to his head like a strange toxic chemical.

The proprietress continued her incessant tour of charm around the café. From somewhere over the wooden partitions came the thick, seductive smell of a cigar, like the smoke of a garden bonfire hanging low over the walls. Her husband went on sculpting the golden chalices of beer, scooping away some of the white froth in order to top up the level, as though each chalice presented its own moral dilemma.

'Let's face it, Herr Doktor Krone, Leipzig is no longer the place for you,' the officer intoned. 'You want to leave your wife, don't you? We're making it easy for you. We're giving you a top job in Berlin. You will be working for peace, for stability, for the democratic socialist ideals. You can forget about everything and start again.'

They drove him back to the university. They were offering him a little more time to think about it, but did not expect to be disappointed. He showed them passive contempt in return. Just before he stepped out of the car, one of the officers discreetly placed the cassette recording into the pocket of his coat. The tape emphasized the shock of his predicament, making everything seem blunt and real. Its existence in his pocket seemed to turn his affair with Christa into a public performance. He could not make up his mind whether to drive home to his wife or go to Christa's apartment and sat in his own car like a mindless dummy. When he eventually switched on the engine the windscreen wipers started up, reminding him of how it had been raining that morning. So much had changed since then. He took out the cassette and placed it in the tape deck. As soon as the words and the images of the previous night began to play back to him, he was struck by a primitive fascination. He heard his own laugh and, with an ominous detachment from the real world, began to laugh along with himself.

SEVEN

Christa Süsskind had no alternative but to sign up with the Stasi as an informal operative. It was a trade-off for her brother, who had been arrested in their home town of Halle for some involvement on the fringes of the smuggling racket with West Germany. The Stasi had been looking for an opportunity to turn her into an informer. They were clever enough not to link it to Ralf Krone, however, and waited till a week after giving him the ultimatum before they bluntly put it to her that her brother would go to Bautzen or Hohenschönhausen. In addition, her application for work in Berlin would go nowhere if she refused to co-operate.

At the time, Christa thought it was no more than a formality. She would make a useless informer. Her deliberate ineptitude would soon put them off. In any case, the idea of storing up banal information about people seemed less serious because, after all, life involved a certain amount of conspiracy as it was. The MfS had merely grafted on another semi-conscious daily act, like the talcum powder that turned her pubic hair momentarily white after a shower, like the sting of perfume between her breasts, or the last-minute look in the mirror.

Her biggest fear was that Ralf might have some connection with the Stasi, that he loved her only in order to use her. He didn't phone. Had he given her up? She began to think it was all over and decided to go home to Halle to be with her mother for a couple of days. The train journey alone through the flat grey landscape was enough to drive her into depression. The emission from the chimneys induced an environmental claustrophobia that underlined her intellectual conscription. Coal dust got into everything. The landscape had lost its innocence.

At home, the sight of her brother Thomas just released from detention reminded her of the power of the MfS. They had kept their promise. She fought back tears of self-pity thinking how she had sold out to the state for him. She told her mother of her intention to go to work in Berlin.

Christa could not force herself to phone Ralf. Even when she got back to Leipzig she was determined to leave it up to him to make the first move. She ultimately became resigned to the fact that it might all have been a short, memorable affair which had come to an abrupt end. When Ralf eventually did phone her at the hospital, it was impossible to talk openly or voice her delight. The compulsion for immediate honesty was gone. He said he had been looking for her; he had something to tell her.

It was early summer. Christa and Ralf agreed to meet at a café close to the university and go for a drive. She was suspicious, even haughty. She could not get over the shock of seeing Ralf; his slightly gaunt appearance, the wave of hair, the roguery in his eyes. Ralf kissed her on the way to the car as though nothing had changed between them, and Christa kept the Stasi business to herself. In the end, there would always be things that a woman kept to herself. She had never talked about her past lovers, or about the abortion she had when she was eighteen. There would always be secrecy.

They drove away, out beyond the city limits of Leipzig into the country.

'Christa, did you tell the Stasi anything about me?' Ralf asked suddenly.

When it finally came, the question shocked her so much that she responded with hostility. She wondered if Ralf knew that the Stasi had conscripted her. But she behaved as though it were a complete surprise. He sounded so innocent.

'What are you asking me, Ralf?'

33

'You know they put a bug in your apartment,' he persisted, slowing down the car to underline the seriousness. 'They read out nearly every word to me. They gave me a cassette, Christa.'

'A cassette, for God's sake?' she echoed, dumbfounded.

She asked him what he had done with it and he assured her that he had destroyed it. It seemed like a question of loyalty. He stopped the car by the side of the road, leaving the engine running until the exhaust fumes began to make their way into the car, choking them. She opened the window, but it only made matters worse. Then he switched the engine off and tinkling contraction sounds began under the bonnet. A passing truck rocked the car.

'Why are they after you, Ralf?' she asked bluntly.

'That's what I wanted to tell you, Christa. I've been given this job in Berlin with the foreign department. I suppose they came to check me out.'

Christa said nothing. She felt ridiculously cramped in the car seat. She had not expected the shock of his departure for Berlin to hit her so hard. She wanted to go with him right away but could not allow herself that obvious dedication to a man.

'You're leaving.'

'I'll be running a science and technology section. You know, I'll be travelling abroad and things like that. I suppose they had to make sure I was clean.'

She fought back her disappointment. Sooner or later everything came to an end, though she had not expected it so soon. He told her to come to Berlin and visit him. But these seemed like empty words.

He took her hand deliberately and clasped it between his. 'I'll miss you, Christa,' he said, starting up the engine again and driving on towards the dark green forest front lines of the Hartz as though there were some great sense of purpose all of a sudden. They could see the hills, already black against the evening sky. The direction in which they travelled together

34

seemed like an unspoken affirmation of their relationship, the motion of the car tacitly stating what nobody could say in words.

They pulled over at the entrance to a wooded path. The light was fading. A sign illuminated in the headlights forbade entry to cars and motorbikes, but Ralf got out, raised the wooden barrier, drove the car in and lowered the barrier behind them; a small transgression against the forestry laws which seemed to increase the silent urgency of their physical longing. He stopped the car further along the path and Christa got out. The headlights lit up her legs, along with the bewildered insects spinning around her.

EIGHT

Mathias took the dog to the kennels. In fact he ended up doing both, first taking Claudia's mother to the train station, making sure she was on the right train and in the right seat, waving her goodbye, and then taking the dog to the kennels in the Wedding district. Claudia said she would make it all worth his while, putting on her Wild West saloon girl act, stroking his chin and blinking with promise.

'Another foot massage?' Mathias remarked.

Werner went with him to have a look at all the other dogs. Outside the kennels they could already hear the sound of barking, and the labrador became nervous and dragged his hind legs. Werner had to pull the lead while Mathias half carried the dog towards the entrance.

'He doesn't want to go,' Werner said.

'He won't mind so much when we get him settled in.'

The woman who ran the kennel wore a black leather jacket, boots and dangling earrings, all of which seemed to give her a masculine appearance. She had a moustache, wore no make-up, and smoked a thin cigar. She made a point of communicating with the dog first, calming him down instantly with a few strokes on the head. Her second objective was to put the owner at ease. She allowed the labrador to investigate the general area before locking him into an enclosure with two other docile pets.

A pungent smell of dog shit competed with a smell of disinfectant. Werner wandered around the kennels, looking at the variety of dogs, enjoying the luxury of watching some deadly biting machines from behind the safety of the wire mesh. He watched a Rottweiler making circles each time before barking at him. The first time, Werner jumped back a little, then he stood closer and observed the dog's teeth, and his snarling upper snout.

'Frau Beniers said her dog was a little strange the last time he came back,' Mathias said, but the kennel owner immediately began to persuade him that the dog had been very happy. It always took them a day or two to adjust back to the apartment environment after being out in the open so long. Dogs also missed the companionship of other dogs, though Mathias didn't think lying around in cages sounded much like companionship. He talked in a joking way about the labrador coming home emotionally disturbed, but the woman took him seriously and became offended. Each dog received the same amount of affection and attention, she insisted.

Werner had moved from greyhounds to Great Danes. Further along the way he found a group of dachshunds and a small corgi which kept whining. At intervals, Mathias kept thinking about his work, especially Christa Süsskind, wondering how he would approach the investigation and wondering too if he wasn't getting sucked into some kind of a time warp with her.

'What happened to your Wall dogs?' he then asked the owner.

'Ah yes, the Wall dogs,' she said, nodding towards the Rottweilers. 'There, I still have two of them. Nobody would buy them. I couldn't put them in with other dogs. I might keep them for breeding.'

'They're not exactly what you would call house pets.'

'Hardly. Most of them were sadly neglected, half dead with thirst in the summer. They were so highly trained. I had four half starved Alsatians as well, but I eventually sold them on to a security company.'

Werner had found a group of puppies and watched them running around biting, fighting, falling over and occasionally receiving a snarl from their mother when they went too far. The kennel owner allowed him in to pet them. On the way home, Werner made another attempt to ask for a puppy. Mathias and Claudia had always put off the issue with a certain ambivalence, not giving in to the request and not wanting to extinguish his interest in animals either. At times Werner still believed he would get a dog. 'I can't wait till we get a dog,' he said occasionally in a kind of fantasy, as though he wasn't expecting an answer any more.

NINE

Claudia went straight from work to meet Alexandra. It was customary for them to have a meal together every second Wednesday, as they had remained good friends ever since university. Since before Claudia had met Mathias, or before Alexandra had met Mathias and passed him on to Claudia. But any notion that Claudia had inherited Mathias from Alexandra had disappeared long ago; it was outweighed by Claudia's feeling that she had got a better deal in husbands and the fact that Claudia and Alexandra had such a durable friendship. There was no secrecy, and no rivalry. They discussed everything together in the complete absence of threat and, if anything, it was Mathias who sometimes became envious of this strong female bond.

Alexandra had chosen a Greek restaurant in Kreuzberg. Since Claudia had made no cooking arrangements at home, she had suggested Mathias should take Werner to his favourite diner on their way back from the kennels. But Mathias and Werner opted for a take-away pizza instead and sat in the kitchen at home watching football.

Against Greek music in the background, Alexandra talked about her recent, brief affair with a Swabian teacher at a counselling conference in Ulm. Claudia still found it hard to believe, even though she had already heard the basic details on the phone. 'I think I just fell in love with his accent. I've no other explanation for it,' Alexandra said.

'Are you going to meet him again?' Claudia wanted to know.

'Are you mad? It wasn't like that. It worked for that short spell, but no, I couldn't go on with it. That would be ridiculous. It was just a fling.'

They examined every detail of the affair: who said what first, who made the initial move, even down to the bedroom tactics. Claudia had often thought about having an affair herself, but there was something in her nature which always worked against it. She didn't have Alexandra's casual attitude towards sex. Nor could she step in and out of people's lives so easily. For Claudia, everything somehow always remained deliberate and meaningful, and though she had an occasional attraction for certain men other than Mathias, it was always accompanied by an instinctive self-analysis, as though she could never stop seeing the end result. She always visualized the inevitable grief. She felt it would require an enormous level of courage even to get it going, and once it was going, how would you stop it? If only she could get drunk and have a blind, transient romance that would play itself out like a brief dream, but her nature dictated everything out of sobriety, or out of some crazy stubbornness.

Claudia and Alexandra usually talked about men in general. They took apart every piece of gossip. Every time some man made a pass at either of them, it underwent an investigation. They discussed everything from fantasies to feminist issues. And when Claudia happened to mention Kevin, the Irishman, it may have come as a response to Alexandra's affair or perhaps out of female solidarity.

'Kevin. Yes, he's fanciable all right,' Alexandra said.

'I would apply that to Ireland in general,' Claudia said. 'I love the place. I'm going to try and get Mathias to go back to Donegal next year.'

'Donegal. *Ach du Liebe!*'

Later, when they went to the Irish pub on Friederich Strasse to meet the others, Claudia exchanged a humorous look with Alexandra as they shook hands with Kevin. Klaus was already there and received a kiss from both women. So too did Stefan and Dieter, dressed in their tight-fitting T-shirts. Alexandra found an opportunity to ask Claudia if she thought Kevin was gay too, but Claudia didn't think so because she said she had received a telling glance from the Irishman already. 'Significant eye contact,' she whispered, and they both laughed.

The pub was a piece of Ireland, imported straight from Derry. The wood, the barmen, the pictures of Irish authors and singers on the walls; sepia-coloured Irish street scenes from long ago and posters advertising Irish breakfast. Over the speakers there was Irish music; some song about a woman's heart. In another corner there was a noisy group of men talking and laughing together, most of them workers from the new building sites of the East. Everybody seemed to know everyone else.

Claudia was struck by Ireland-fever. Berlin soon became a small enclave of Ireland. When Mathias arrived she embraced him and said how she wanted to go to Donegal. It seemed almost like a proposal of love and was spoken in the same tones she might have used in the bedroom. Mathias joked and asked her how much Guinness she had already consumed. But then he admitted that it had been on his mind too.

'We've got to go back,' Claudia declared in perfect English. She vowed to get out all the photographs when she got home. They talked about Ireland as though they knew more about it than Kevin or any other Irish person in the bar. Alexandra and Klaus began to talk about the two mountains they had come across in Co. Kerry which looked like breasts when the sunset lit up the pagan tumulus on each summit like nipples.

Mathias ordered more drinks. Somebody tried Kilkenny beer and Kevin told the apocryphal marketing legend about the beer's original name, 'Smithwicks', being so consumer-unfriendly in Germany. Claudia didn't immediately understand why, and Mathias explained quietly that in German it sounded a bit like '*Schmidt-vix*', or 'Smith wanks'. It was followed by a string of similar brand-name follies from Japan to Moscow and Mathias was inspired to mention the East German imitation of Coca-Cola. Because the German word for fizz in soft drinks was *prickeln*, it had been marketed during GDR times under the name of 'Prick Cola'.

When Kevin suddenly asked Claudia if she had ever been to Doolin, she placed her hand on her heart and sighed: 'Doolin.' Of course they had been there. Mathias recalled how he had been mistaken for the footballer Rudi Voller. Everybody's Ireland experience had to be retold in ecstatic tones. Claudia then remembered the Irish tissues and began to talk passionately about this symbol of gender discrimination in Ireland.

'Imagine, man-size tissues,' she said.

'I don't believe it,' Alexandra said.

'I'm serious. I couldn't get over it. I always thought that, at least with noses, men and women were basically equal,' she said.

A guitarist and a woman singer began to perform a haunting emigration song in the corner. Claudia showed open affection towards Mathias; her arm was around his back, her head leaning against his shoulder. These memories of Ireland suddenly brought back all the original feelings of love for Mathias, as though they were back in Clare or Mayo or Donegal on that first holiday, before they were married. At one point she announced that they were going to have a party. On the wave of Ireland hysteria, it seemed like a great idea, even though she had said nothing to Mathias about it beforehand. With the sound of the singing in the background, Mathias backed her up, pretending that they had been planning it for some time. But there was a misunderstanding, because Mathias had assumed she meant having the party in the garden house when Claudia really meant having it at home in the apartment. For once, they were almost on the same wavelength.

TEN

The following day Mathias drove along Hallesches Ufer on his way to meet Christa Süsskind in order to bring her to Hohenschönhausen prison. He could see the yellow U-Bahn darting above him until it stopped at the next station and he sped on in his car. He passed close by the former Polish flea market, where the people from the East used to gather to sell their wares. He recalled the Polish buses after the Wall came down, blue with cigarette smoke, packed with the anxious faces of passengers carrying ghetto-blasters, TVs and other Western goods on their knees all the way back to Warsaw. All that initial panic buying seemed to have died down now.

He collected Christa at a café near Alexanderplatz, hardly recognizing her since their meeting in his office. She was dressed more conventionally, wearing a blue skirt with white hieroglyphic patterns and a light grey jacket. She appeared a little nervous.

'God, it's like a sauna,' she said.

'I hope I didn't keep you waiting.'

She took off her jacket before stepping into the car and only partly gathered her skirt underneath her. The idea of her bare legs making direct contact with the leather of the car seat fired Mathias's male imagination; he was reminded once more of how good she looked and how she had immediately begun to stimulate more than his journalistic interest. She seemed glad of the air-conditioning and began to lift the collar of her blouse. He asked himself if Claudia would still look as well in five or ten years time.

'Do I look all right?' she asked. He was caught off-balance a little and only then began to realize her apprehension.

'Great, absolutely perfect,' he said. 'It shouldn't take long.'

'I'm afraid,' she admitted. 'I've never been back there. I don't know if it's going to make me feel better or worse.'

'You'll be fine. It may be a bit of a shock. But we'll only stay as long as you want to.'

They could have made the journey to the prison with the photographer, but Mathias had decided to travel alone with her, in case she might want to talk. She seemed reluctant to reveal much about her experiences, though she volunteered some peculiar information, saying that she had once met her partner Ralf inside the prison. They had been brought together and watched. But as soon as she mentioned this she began to get nervous and appeared to withdraw what she had just said. She didn't want any of these things published.

Mathias had studied the engrained reticence of the East Germans; their lack of confidence stemmed from a lingering feeling of inferiority towards the West. They had not yet discovered the sense of dignity which derived from money and maintained a clandestine attitude towards shopping. In supermarkets they returned fierce, dirty looks instead of smiling and apologizing for crashing into your ankles with their trolleys. And when you said something, they would shrink back at the slightest voice of authority. The highly advanced culture of complaint in the West left them silent with their primitive sense of self-justice. Silence had become an evolutionary over-specialization under socialism; the New Forum intellectual Jens Reich had spoken of East Germans as oysters, their greatest strength being in their closing muscle.

Mathias felt he needed an oyster knife with Christa. Or was she more sophisticated than that? Was she stringing him along perhaps? She talked more freely about her job with the dentist. She could never quite shake off the whine of the drill in her ears and didn't enjoy being a symbol of pain; it made her feel a bit like a terrorist.

44

Outside the grey gate of the prison, Christa looked around at the watchtowers and the security cameras, all abandoned and frozen in time. She had never seen the outside of the prison. The small, stocky photographer was already waiting for them, dressed completely out of context in shorts and a colourful T-shirt. He shook hands and eyed Christa up and down, telling her she looked beautiful. It was part of a photographer's repertoire, the verbal anaesthetic.

The caretaker arrived and unlocked the side gate. But before he led them inside he asked them to turn around and look at the canyons of apartment blocks around the area. 'All Stasi,' the caretaker said. 'Everywhere you look. They were all, and still are all, Stasi. Nobody wants to move into this area now. Look, this road here was never on the map; it's not even on the new map today.'

Inside, in the open, weed-covered concrete yard of the prison, Christa looked around as though she had never been there before either. A wreath had been placed on a wall in honour of those who had suffered under the system here, from the KGB right down to the Stasi. The caretaker pointed to the seamless transition between the Nazi regime and the new socialist terror. He talked about the latest plans to turn Hohenschönhausen into a museum of Stalinist oppression.

'Jesus, there will be nothing but museums around Germany,' the photographer muttered.

They walked through the staff buildings first, through the ransacked Stasi offices. The photographer picked up a newspaper dated 15 January 1990. Christa hardly spoke at all, everything entering into her consciousness like slow-releasing shock. She spoke openly for the first time when they entered an area of what looked like small dog pounds. 'I was here,' she said, looking up at the wire grid roof and the guard ramp above it. 'This was the exercise yard.'

Mathias was anxious to get the photographs over with quickly. They made their way to the building in which she had been kept.

45

The doors had been left open as though all the inmates had suddenly fled together like pigeons. Paper cards with their numbers were still attached to the outside of the doors, and the inside of the cells were beige halfway up, with a thin pink line separating it from the white. There wasn't one mark on the walls; not a scrawl or a single piece of graffiti. The guards always shouted, she recalled. You were never allowed to see them. You never knew anyone's name. You were not allowed to speak. She talked about the red lights at the end of each corridor. You never saw or heard another prisoner.

At the entrance to her own cell, she became even more introspective. The photographer tried to relax her with his professional patter, cracking crass little jokes to deflect her attention. 'You're gorgeous, my love,' he kept saying. 'Just lovely. One more by the door, for my aunt in Dortmund.'

This was the cell in which she had spent most of her detention. Christa stared at the bunk bed and the grey blankets, smelling the familiar mildewed stench. 'There was only a wooden bunk when I was here,' she said. 'And there was no basin or mirror then.'

The photographer asked her if she could recline on the bunk. He wanted a natural shot of her lying back.

'That won't be necessary,' Mathias said, sensing her discomfort.

Mathias cautiously began to put some questions to her. He wanted to know how she was treated and whether she had gone from Hohenschönhausen straight to a maternity hospital. Could she remember the travelling time between there and where she gave birth to the baby? They were all vital questions. He was hoping that the shock of this sudden exposure to the past would bring back more details.

It was chilly inside the prison buildings and she rubbed her arms, staring at the circled lino pattern in the corridor. One of the few comments she made spontaneously referred to her work in the kitchens.

'I used to put an extra piece of meat on one plate every day, just hoping it would get to Ralf . . .'

Mathias accompanied her slowly around the prison. The photographer had left. The caretaker said he would wait for them outside and, now that the fear of Hohenschönhausen had been overcome, Christa seemed interested in looking around; she was suddenly gripped by a perverse fascination for the place. It was so strange to think of its being so empty. Once or twice she mentioned the name of Erwin Pückler, but generally she seemed lost in a trance of subjective memory. Mathias brought her down to the famous 'U-Boot' section where inmates were held underground in complete darkness for long periods of time. She had never been here herself, but she wanted to know everything about it.

Finally they came to the interrogation rooms on the first floor.

'This is where they watched us,' she said.

'You mean you and Ralf?' Mathias asked.

'Me, Ralf and everyone else, I suppose,' she said, approaching the mirror and staring at herself.' There was a bed there in the corner. They could see us through this. Then they shot him.'

'You witnessed that?' he asked.

'No,' she said instantly. She looked at Mathias as if to see how much she could trust him.

'How do you know he's dead then?'

She hesitated and looked around the room again, pointing to the place where she remembered two chairs, ignoring his question.

'How do you know they shot him?' he asked again.

'That's what I was told,' she said after a moment. 'Pückler: he told me that.'

The adjacent room contained some desks and a filing cabinet. Everything had been left the way it was in January 1990. Christa went over to look through the one-way mirror, back at the room they had just come from. She asked Mathias if he wouldn't mind

47

going back inside for a few minutes. He obliged her and went back into the room next door where she observed him walking around, unable to see her.

ELEVEN

Claudia was in a slightly cool mood when Mathias got home.
They had not resolved their disagreement over whether to hold
the party at the apartment or out in the garden house. The truth
was that Mathias would have preferred to drop the idea of a
party altogether, but Claudia had committed herself to a particular date already. For her it was a big event. Mathias had other big
events in his life, or in his work. Claudia was fed up with
barbecues. She wanted people to dress up, and wanted a reason
to buy something new herself. Out there in the garden everyone
would turn up in shorts and T-shirts. She wanted style.

The issue simmered all evening without any conclusion.
Mathias talked about the visit to the prison, dramatizing certain
details, but Claudia wasn't really listening. It was only late at
night when they addressed the subject of the party that she
became more responsive.

'For God's sake, Claudia, it's the summer. It's only logical to
have it in the garden,' he argued.

'Don't be crazy. You can't have a party in the garden. This
should be a real party with a bit of flair. In any case, I've already
started telling people to come here.'

'*Scheisse!*' he said. 'Tell them you made a mistake, it's at the
garden.'

She leaned forward and her dressing gown fell open, revealing
her breasts. When Mathias again pleaded with her that it was
more practical to have the party in the open where the neighbours would not be disturbed, she became furious, throwing her

arms up. Her breasts shook. If she'd wanted a garden party, she would have said so.

'Matt, what is wrong with you?' she said, gathering herself together again. 'I would like to invite people to the apartment. It would give me a nice feeling to live in a place which is used for social occasions now and then.'

'It would be a better party out there. Everyone could stay late and make lots of noise,' Mathias said.

'*Scheisse!*' she said. 'We're not communicating. You just don't want to understand.'

She stood up and began to pace up and down the living room. She was vaguely aware that they were raising their voices and that people in other apartments could hear the argument drifting through the open windows into the courtyard. Werner was unable to sleep with the noise and came out of his room in his pyjamas. His mother told him to go back to bed, everything was fine. She would come in and say goodnight.

Claudia began to try again. She was determined to introduce more fun into her life. Her voice started once more at its lowest, most reasonable pitch, trying to persuade Mathias that an apartment had a soul, and that the soul of your living space had to be rejuvenated with the voices and laughter of other people.

'Matt, I want there to be laughter and fun here again.'

Mathias smiled in derision at all this soul talk. The argument sank too low to make any more sense. Claudia gave up and stormed out of the room into the kitchen, slamming the door behind her. Werner came out again to see what had happened and Mathias began to explain that Claudia was being completely unreasonable. He raised his voice so that Claudia could hear what he was saying, speaking indirectly at her and distorting everything to his own ends.

'She's insane. She wants to bring half of Berlin in here. All these alternative freaks, people who will never invite us back in a million years. She wants to fill all these assholes with food and drink too.'

Mathias knew he was being unreasonable. There was a moment of silence where he and Werner waited for a response from behind the kitchen door. Nothing. Mathias recalled how his own father had once, under the influence of alcohol, shot a hole through the kitchen door with his hunting gun. The same door was still there, with the new diamond-shaped piece of wood set in to hide the hole. Compared with that, Mathias felt he was even-tempered. He put his hand on Werner's shoulder and began to lead him back towards his bedroom.

'And now she's in there stuffing her face with biscuits,' he shouted over his shoulder.

He could not pass up the triumph of speaking the last word. It occurred to him that it was a very male thing, that compulsion to have the final say. In many ways, he realized, he was no different from his father, only he wasn't using a gun.

TWELVE

The Christa Süsskind piece appeared two days later on the inside pages of the *Tageszeitung*. Ironically, it appeared beside a small item reporting two separate muggings on the same night in Berlin, one using a hammer and the other a sickle. The picture showed Christa holding the grey door of her cell, with its heavy black bolts, peephole and food hatch. In the background, the polished institutional lino reflected the overhead neon lights along the corridor. She was neither smiling nor serious, just bearing an unforced look of accusation. The caption read: 'HOHENSCHONHAUSEN – PRISONER OF THE PAST.'

Mathias had selected this particular shot himself. But it was not until it appeared in the paper, not until she had somehow been extruded through the newsprint medium, that he felt the full visual force of her looks. She's really something, he thought. As he held the paper with her photograph in his hands he felt she belonged to him.

'WHERE IS CHRISTA'S BABY?' ran the headline across the top of the story. It gave a brief outline of the events in her life along with the assumption that her partner Ralf Krone had been executed in Hohenschönhausen. The report gave a description of her present circumstances: 'the former GDR nurse from Halle, now working for a Moabit dentist, is concerned that her past at the hands of the Stasi is met only by apathy . . .'

He had employed emotive language and wondered if he should be devoting so much time and effort to her story. There was a low tolerance in Germany for stories of this kind, and the media had all but lost interest, preferring the more urgent headlines of racial attacks and right-wing fervour. Mathias had recently been reporting on deportation flights: a passenger in Frankfurt had slashed himself and his wife to avoid repatriation; there was blood all over Lufthansa.

And yet Mathias continued his investigation into Christa's past with unprecedented enthusiasm. He found time to sit in the records offices, conducting searches in the births register, checking through the lists of patients at Berlin hospitals. He went on the trail of ex-MfS people from Normannen Strasse, revisiting the 'Mielke Suite', looking for traces of Erwin Pückler in particular. But he seemed to have disappeared altogether. It had been impossible even to put together a list of Stasi personnel at Hohenschönhausen prison.

Christa was not so pleased with the article. She had not expected Mathias to be so blunt in the copy. 'What has the dentist got to do with it?' she accused. The publicity had led to nuisance calls at the dentist's surgery, from pornographers and conmen out to target East European women. A man sat in a parked car outside the surgery for a whole day.

Mathias promised that he would not print another word without her consent. And once again, he wondered whether he should leave the people of East Germany to sort out their own problems with the past. He suggested to Christa that she should apply for her Stasi file and arranged to drive her over to the Gauk Institut, responsible for managing this Stasi inheritance, which extended to 200 kilometres of files. In his presence, she was politely informed that she would not be entitled to any information on her former partner Ralf Krone. Any references to him would be deleted from the file.

'Typical Gauk logic,' Mathias said to her later when they stopped for coffee. 'Doesn't make sense, protecting the dead, does it?'

Christa didn't comment.

53

'You were classified under operational file,' he said. 'Did you sign an agreement with the Stasi?'

'I had no alternative,' she snapped back. Then she fell silent and began to watch a tram filling up with passengers in the distance.

'You have no idea,' she said at last. 'They were holding my brother, Thomas. They were going to give him ten years in Bautzen. What could I do?'

'I understand, Fräulein Süsskind. I'm only trying to help you to get all the facts straight. But why are the Gauk withholding the information on Ralf? Were you meant to inform on him?'

'I told them nothing new,' she said. 'Jesus, this is like being interrogated.'

THIRTEEN

Claudia eventually got round Mathias. On the evening of the party the guests began to arrive at six in the evening, and by seven the apartment was packed. The furniture had been pushed back towards the walls and the larger of the sofas had been moved into the main bedroom. Werner's room became a cloak-room; he was staying with Mathias's parents. Claudia and Alexandra had hung up balloons everywhere, and on the seventeenth-century oak trunk in the hallway stood a bottle of champagne, a glass and a single red high-heeled shoe. People were already using the bookshelves to rest their glasses on and somebody was half sitting on the Iroquois sculpture. Claudia announced that everyone should help themselves to food. When the babble of conversation resumed, nobody could hear the music, so she forced a path through the centre of the living room in order to switch it off, smiling at everyone in passing.

On her way back she met Mathias with two plates of food in his hands, reluctantly playing the good host. She blew him a silent kiss and asked him to check the garlic bread. Alexandra was going around with the wine, white and red, chatting to the guests, introducing people from the media to the people from the American Express bank where Claudia worked. She was dressed in a bottle-green dress with underwiring that displayed her bosom. Klaus was wearing his red and white striped jacket.

Dieter tried to capture the events on his video, but gave it up when he got nothing more than a series of close-ups of ears and noses. Klaus stuck his tongue out at the camera. The guests were mixed; half Claudia's friends and half Mathias's. There was a tall, bony-looking woman standing beside the Tai Chi instructor, and the financial reporter of the *Tageszeitung* was being savaged in a conversation about 'Meat is murder' which soon evolved into an argument on biotechnology. Someone asked Claudia if that was her in a painting they had by a famous Berlin artist, and Claudia nodded: 'But I don't look like that any more.' The painting was more like a random splash of various colours. Claudia then managed to introduce a young artist friend to the arts editor of the *Tageszeitung* and felt she had done a good deed.

She met Kevin standing by the open window with one of his Irish friends. She smiled at them and asked if they had had any of the food yet. Perhaps she was already paying special attention to Kevin, she thought. There was something about him. Every time she came near him she became self-conscious, as though she should be giving him a wide berth in case he might say something intimate to her.

'Don't fall out there,' she said to them.

'Don't you worry,' Kevin said, looking down into the court-yard.' It's like the Cliffs of Moher down there.'

She laughed, but felt she had lingered there too long already. 'The Cliffs of Moher without the seagulls,' she said. Claudia wore a new backless dress made of light blue crêpe de Chine, hugging her body and barely reaching beyond her bottom. For the first time, the dress felt short. She picked up an ashtray and made her way back towards the kitchen, wondering how much she was showing from behind.

Mathias was talking to his colleague Max Rodiger in the hallway. Max had just handed him the key to his apartment in Kreuzberg and asked him to find a good tenant.

'If you find somebody in the short term, Matt . . .'

'I'll put up a note at the office,' Mathias said. They talked for a while about Max's new USA assignment. Then Max wanted to know if there had been any progress on Christa Süsskind.

'She was an operative,' Mathias told him. 'The whole thing is a bit of a mess. And her partner seems to have been executed. So there's not much to go on.'

Alexandra came running out of the kitchen with a box of salt. Claudia followed her, and when they returned some minutes later Claudia smiled triumphantly at Mathias to indicate that it was one of his friends who had spilled the wine on the carpet. Most of the journalists seemed to be gathering in the hallway, beside the bathroom, where they could talk to everyone waiting in the queue, making private comments. One of the *Tageszeitung* people had gone into Werner's room to start playing with the computer games. Claudia spoke to Mathias about it, saying it was very ill-mannered but typically *Tageszeitung*. Claudia allowed special people into the en-suite bathroom in the main bedroom.

The party had come to a high point when everybody seemed involved in conversation everywhere. The foreign editor had got talking to the Irishmen. The music was on again in the background and Claudia wondered why they didn't have parties more often.

The journalists were the only guests who ate the cake. They also seemed to be winning on stamina when the bony woman and her husband left early, followed by some of their health-conscious apostles. Even Claudia said she was a bit pissed off with their lack of endurance. With the extra space, she and Alexandra started off the dancing and Klaus instantly worked himself into a sweat. His cravat was hanging out of his top pocket and he danced with his eyes closed. The Irishmen headed for the safety of the kitchen, remarking that Irish people only had the use of their lower limbs, from the hips down; a Catholic inheritance. Dancing was Satanic. Somebody became possessed and did a cross between Tai Chi and Michael Jackson. The foreign editor had cement feet and staggered a little.

Everybody was hot. There was condensation on the windows and beads of perspiration on everyone's faces. At one point, just when Claudia was in the kitchen, leaning into the fridge to get some mineral water, she felt a firm slap on her bottom. She sprang up and saw Klaus standing behind her. He had followed her into the kitchen for some water. She was angry with him. The incident was over within seconds, but Mathias had seen it from his position in the hallway and, after her initial show of anger, Claudia found herself less concerned with the slap than with Mathias's reaction. Kevin happened to be there too, which made it much worse. But when she saw that Mathias appeared to be looking away, deep in a conversation on European monetary union, she laughed and picked up a dishcloth which she began to push up towards Klaus's face.

Eventually, when only the inner core of friends and professional colleagues were left, Alexandra persuaded Mathias and Max Rodiger to join in the dancing. One of the journalists was still eating, but at one stage everybody was on the floor and the party reached an intimate climax of bodies shaking and jumping around. Alexandra and Claudia were colliding against each other's hips and Mathias kept joking about hip replacements.

The music ended punctually, shortly after half past ten. Somebody suggested getting into a taxi and going out somewhere to keep dancing all night, but then Claudia remembered the champagne. Who was going to drink from the red stiletto, she asked. They all laughed and accused her of offering them a smelly old shoe. But then Klaus volunteered, and, though Mathias tried to diminish his gallantry by saying that Klaus would drink champagne from any old football boot, Claudia applauded.

It was Kevin who suddenly asked if there was a guitar around, and everybody looked at him as though he had asked for a set of rosary beads or an orgy. Nobody had had that notion since they were all in summer camp. The idea caught on immediately.

'Now we're going live,' Claudia said with some excitement, holding the champagne bottle like a microphone. Mathias got the old Spanish guitar from the spare room while Claudia closed the windows to contain any further noise.

Kevin sang a ballad and everyone listened in amazement, not merely at the sound of his singing, but at the conviction with which he took over from the recorded music. It seemed to come straight from the heart. Claudia sat down beside Mathias, examining each word coming from Kevin's mouth with astonishment. His eyes were closed as he sang, and suddenly everyone felt sad and hopelessly introspective. It proved how music really was the fastest way to the brain, faster than love, faster than champagne. There was long applause.

He had to sing another one. And when Kevin began to fling himself passionately into the next song, this time with his eyes open, Claudia felt he was staring straight up her dress, along the tunnel created by her thighs. She pulled her legs up towards Mathias on the sofa.

Then everyone looked around for a successor. Claudia asked Mathias to sing, but he said it was years since he had held the guitar in his hand. Kevin's friend began to sing an unaccompanied song about the 'Croppy Boy', and when it finally ended someone said Germans were inadequate, that they had lost the ability to sing.

'Claudia, would you know where the music is?' Mathias said, finally capitulating. Claudia went to the filing cabinet in the spare room to get a folder which she brought back and opened out on her knees, decisively cutting out any further view of the tunnel.

Mathias first tried a number of chords on the guitar. Then he began with one Neil Young song after another, going on systematically through until he reached Bob Dylan. It was as though he had to outdo the Irishman's performance, as though he was trying to regain Claudia's admiration. People clapped for the first one, but then it seemed too much like a revision exercise. Eventually Mathias found a song where everyone could join in wholeheartedly, despite the German accent leaning heavily on the words: 'Good morning America how are you . . .'

FOURTEEN

Christa Süsskind's Stasi file became available. When Mathias got
a look at it he was surprised that, apart from the sections blacked
out deliberately by the Gauk Institut to protect Ralf Krone, there
were other parts of the file missing. Substantial chunks of the
document seemed to have been deleted. Over the phone, he was
able to establish that the missing sections had disappeared
during the Stasi period; they had never been found anywhere,
either in Leipzig or in Berlin. Christa Süsskind suspected Erwin
Pückler, though why he would need to suppress parts of this file
remained a mystery.

Mathias decided it would be essential to interview her once
more, perhaps on a less formal basis, in a bar somewhere.

'Do you think you could find Kotbusser Tor on the U-Bahn?'
he asked.

'Don't underestimate my talents, Herr Hauser,' she said, and
he was surprised by her spontaneous sense of humour.

He gave her directions to a bar close by the station. In the
meantime, he examined the file carefully for any clues. He had
talked to many other people about their Stasi files: meticulous
records of dullness containing every word, every family row,
every command to the dog. What assailed people in former East
Germany most was not the omnipotence of Stasi surveillance but
the hideous idea of looking back at the banality of their own
lives – the Saturday morning arguments, the moods, the cloying
expressions of family hope, even the imperfections of love.
Nobody wanted to be exposed to their own past in such a blunt

and merciless way. Everyone's own memory was usually far more selective, more kind, more positive. The Stasi people were interested in everything, even the most boring aspects of life, particularly in failure. They were interested in marriage, love, breakdowns, family strife, infidelity – anything which would present them with human vulnerability. Inadvertently, they had left behind the most comprehensive sociological document on any modern society. They were not unlike the camcorder generation in the West, who spent whole weekends filming their kids getting in and out of the car. The most recorded race in history.

Christa could not read through her file. She said it made her sick, even thinking about some of the details. Mathias read through the testimony of waiters, taxi drives and caretakers; anyone who had ever seen Christa Süsskind and Ralf Krone together. Christa's own reports were blacked out, and in all her file revealed nothing new. Mathias was disappointed. The only progress he had made so far was to compile a list of some ex-Hohenschönhausen inmates.

That afternoon Christa made her way by U-Bahn to meet him, getting off at Kotbusser Tor and descending the concrete steps. A young punk girl stretched out her hand to beg a few marks, her face reddened by the sun, hair matted and filthy. In the late afternoon warmth, young men lay on the concrete, some laughing like halfwits through stained teeth, some drinking cans of beer while others slept in a narcotic coma like their docile dogs. One of them lying under the U-Bahn bridge had his trousers open, exposing everything. The salty stench of urine hit her nostrils.

Not far away, Mathias was waiting for her, in a trendy Kreuzberg bar. He wore an open-necked shirt and denim jacket, signalling a more informal attitude. Outside, people sat around the tables under the canopy.

'A bit over-cool,' Christa remarked, pointing her hand at two men in black cycling shorts entering the bar on roller skates.

'Agreed,' Mathias said. He looked a little out of place himself among the slick shapes and pony tails. Christa counted at least three young men with John Lennon glasses and Mathias reminded her that they also doubled as Heinrich Himmler glasses. He wasn't sure if she got the joke.

Mathias began by asking her what she would do if she found the baby. The child would be fourteen years old now. Would she ask for the child to be returned to her?

'Yes, of course. I want the best for my child. It's my right. I don't know what kind of Stasi creeps my child is with, Herr Hauser.'

'Mathias,' he put in. 'Why don't we drop the formalities?'

'Mathias,' she said, gingerly. 'I think it's only fair that I should have the right to see my child. All of these years I have imagined what my child looks like. Every Christmas . . . I don't even know if it's a boy or a girl.'

Mathias decided to abandon this line of questioning since it produced such a strong emotional response. Instead he told her what enquiries he had made. The search through the maternity records of former GDR hospitals was futile, unless he had something more concrete to go on. He showed her the list of inmates. She recognized nobody. The only new information she could offer him was that her brother Thomas had also joined the Stasi as an operative at the same time as her.

'They played the two of us off against each other. They made me sign because of him and they made him sign because of me.'

'And what about Ralf, was he in with them too?'

'Yes, but he was an official member of the MfS, in the science division.'

Mathias went through a list of questions which he had put together from his reading of the file. Christa looked around rather furtively, perhaps because the analysis of her past seemed entirely at odds with this trendy enclave of Berlin. Reticence took over again. She became distracted, watching the people at the bar, answering only in staccato phrases.

Mathias didn't want to keep her too long. He wanted her to feel comfortable with the pace of the investigation and talked about the way in which he would proceed from here. He was still hoping to get some response from the article in the *Tageszeitung*. He wondered if he should volunteer something about himself as a way of encouraging trust. If only he could confess something to her. He told her he would have to go and collect his son in Alt Mariendorf, and this sudden display of personal information on his part seemed to interest her. She wanted to know how old his son was. And what his name was.

'My wife leaves all the ferrying to me,' he said.

Christa smiled. The fleeting glimpse of his life seemed to make her a little more open. She became more talkative and seemed willing to speak about herself again. The fact that he had spoken of his own wife had removed any ambiguities over this meeting, to himself as much as to Christa. He was interested in her. He liked the way she looked. He liked her slightly old-fashioned, Soviet sense of dignity, her silent maturity, her vulnerability and the genuine shyness or lack of pre-emptive sophistication which he associated with Western women. Meeting her casually like this in Kreuzberg, it had crossed his mind that he could become fond of her and that she might test his loyalty towards Claudia. But he had now fully restored his sincerity by mentioning his wife and family. This meeting was strictly professional.

'Tell me about Ralf Krone,' Mathias said. 'Were you going to get married?'

'We never talked about it.'

Mathias probed her further about her relationship with Ralf. He was curious to know what it was like to live in the GDR. He wanted to know how people could trust each other. Christa looked puzzled.

'Look, it's not as though we didn't have fun, you know.'

FIFTEEN

Ralf Krone took up his new position at the MfS technical bureau with little enthusiasm. He left his wife and travelled to Berlin to start his new life under a cloud of guilt, despising the sly way in which he had extracted himself from his marriage. In addition, it kept raining almost incessantly for the first few weeks in Berlin, inducing a state of lethargic withdrawal which made it seem as if it were raining inside his head.

He had brought very little with him from Leipzig, not even his car. The brief trip home to Erfurt to see his parents had weighed him down with enough cutlery to start a canteen. The MfS had assured him that the state would look after all the essentials, but apart from one threadbare towel in the bathroom he found nothing in his new apartment except a pile of newspapers in the wardrobe and a series of grey shadows, around the door handles, around light switches, on the wall behind the bed.

They had given him a new car: a Polish-assembled Fiat. And his new apartment was more spacious than any he'd ever had before. But this generosity, along with the warm welcome from Herr Stanjek and his new MfS colleagues, only added to his self-hatred. He missed Christa.

As the weeks went by, Ralf ultimately found his only redemption in work. Committing his energies to the new science and technology division, he found a degree of liveliness running through the MfS operation which he had witnessed nowhere else before in the GDR. At least in the secret police there was something happening. There was mystique attached to working on classified documents. And the office was located in a comfortable, quiet, detached house on Niebergall Strasse, not in the Normannen Strasse headquarters as he had feared.

His workforce consisted of six men and two women who set about transcribing documents stolen in West Germany under the Marcus Wolf spying operation; documents from all the big firms like Siemens, AG Telefunken, Thyssen, which were made to look as if they originated in East German institutions. But apart from one or two peculiar items from Opel, like the document on colour-obsolescence in cars, it was all boring, second-hand stuff. And the notion that new colours could reduce the value of older models seemed utterly fantastic in the GDR. Very soon, however, Ralf received praise for the speed with which industries in the East could assimilate information extracted from the West.

Luckily, one of the men at work turned out to have come from the same town as Ralf. Rainer Krombholz, a corpulent and jolly character, even said he half remembered Ralf from school. They struck up an immediate, easygoing companionship. There was little else to do in the GDR, other than maintain friendships. Rainer Krombholz was deputy head of the department, a man who enjoyed his food too much to be a threat to anyone. They both drank beer and spent their evenings in the bars, soon confiding to each other how they had been conscripted into the MfS in the first place. Krombholz had been an electrical specialist in Dresden when they caught him.

'I was making a bit of money on the side, recycling electrical equipment,' Krombholz ventured. 'You know yourself, sharing out the national resources among the people, myself mostly. Then I found myself having these nice conversations with people in leather jackets. I didn't like the idea of Bautzen, so signed up for this.'

Ralf told Krombholz his own story.

'An affair with a young woman? *Schwein!*' Krombholz said. 'At least you've got something to remember.'

Stanjek and other leading Stasi members from Normannen

Strasse occasionally phoned or came to visit Ralf in the office. Stanjek made sure not only that the work was going well but that Ralf was integrating socially. He invited him out to meet other state officials, but Ralf discouraged these exalted connections. He preferred to drink beer with Krombholz. He accepted invitations to dinner at home with Krombholz and his wife Mareille, just to watch these overweight people eating and rekindle his own appetite for food. Mareille Krombholz mothered him.

From time to time Stanjek would take Ralf Krone across into West Berlin to a technological exhibition. There would be many more Western projects, Stanjek assured him. West Berlin, with all its colour and excitement, seemed to fill Ralf's imagination, but he never seriously thought of fleeing during these excursions. He felt more of an urge to settle down where he was.

His loyalty and enthusiasm were rewarded some weeks later when he was asked to prepare for an exhibition on fibre-optics in Hamburg. He received a special travel permit signed by Erich Mielke, the Stasi boss himself.

During these intital months Ralf had one brief, unhappy affair with a married woman named Brigitte Geibel whom he met in Potsdam. He had gone out on the S-Bahn to visit the palace of Sanssouci when he fell into conversation with her, admiring the way the giant oak trees had been shaped into hedges. Her husband had gone over to the other side of the estate with their two children and she allowed herself to get lost in the grounds with Ralf. The affair only lasted two weeks. After that he seemed to lose all interest in women. He could only think of Christa Süsskind.

Ralf travelled to Hamburg with his colleague Rainer Krombholz. They both declared themselves to be out for a good time. They conducted their research and drew up their reports by day, making the most of Western nightlife after work. It was the first time Ralf had ever eaten Greek food. The first time he had been into bars with live music. The first time he had seen men in baseball caps singing American Country music.

Krombholz had been to Hamburg before and knew exactly where to go, cautiously suggesting a trip to the Reeperbahn, wondering what kind of attitude Ralf Krone had towards sex. When there was no more space left in their stomachs for food or drink, Ralf allowed himself to be led through some of the sex shops. He watched Rainer greedily picking through the magazines and videos. Ralf found himself going through a rack of magazines featuring anal sex with pure anatomical fascination. Was this what the West was all about, he wondered. Pornography suddenly seemed to offer the most peculiar sense of freedom, as though here he had found the full, unabridged truth which Soviet society had always suppressed. The photography was generally very poor and the women looked as though they were all about to sneeze. But nobody was hiding anything, for once.

Krombholz came over and grabbed three or four magazines from the stand.

'You can make a bit of money on these. Bring back a few and sell them, you know,' Krombholz said. He wore a crown of sweat around his forehead.

'Look, it's all right,' Ralf said awkwardly. 'I don't mind.'

They ended up at a live sex show where two South American women in bikinis came and sat beside them. 'Buy me a Picolo, love,' was all the German they could speak, and Ralf found himself buying four tiny bottles of champagne at extraordinary expense. Krombholz brought one of the women back to the hotel with him.

'I only get pleasure from sex when it's paid for,' he proclaimed in the taxi on the way home. The true capitalist.

Ralf spent the following morning buying sensible things: new shirts, underwear, shaving lotion. Indeed, he was more shocked by the opulence of department stores along the Ku Damm than by the surfeit of sexual images and red lighting clinging to his mind. He thought of Christa. He thought of sending her a card, and in a great rush of excitement went and bought her a pair of black silk briefs. He packed them in a small padded envelope along with a plain card on which he wrote: 'Just because . . .' He put his new Berlin address on the back of the package. He did not sign the card or put any name on it.

SIXTEEN

Back in Berlin, Ralf's work became increasingly routine. He was exasperated by his inability to make things happen in a scientific field; many of his recommendations for industrial regeneration in East Germany had been totally ignored, languishing on shelves. At the same time, the spying operation in the West could not meet the demand for new scientific material.

'Every graduate in the GDR knows this stuff off by heart,' Ralf remarked in the office one day when they received dossiers on basic quantum physics.

He cautiously balanced his overt comments by doing favours for his staff. He managed to get them opera tickets. He got a new car for Krombholz and even put in a good word for the secretary's sister, who had applied to study medicine in Munich. Stanjek was eager to keep Ralf happy and arranged the transport of his old piano from Erfurt. For a while, music turned Ralf into a self-sufficient soul.

Then, one day, a parcel arrived from Christa. Ralf tore the paper away violently and found a pair of dark green socks and a small card on which she had written: 'Just because . . .'

He didn't know whether to be insulted or delighted. Two days later she phoned, and he realized only then that she had sent the parcel from Berlin. 'You're here,' he said with unconcealed excitement. She began to explain how she had found a job in an old people's home in Berlin. 'I missed you,' she said.

He was dizzy that afternoon when he went to meet her at Alexanderplatz. He was there almost half an hour early. It was humid. Not a breath of air moved in the vast open space, and when she finally appeared he hardly recognized her.

'Professor Krone,' she said, leaning forward for a kiss.

He embraced her, crushing her body against his, then holding her out at arm's length to look at her. He showered her with questions, hungry to know everything. He brought her to a bar just off Alexanderplatz, full of men in uniform with their hats laid beside their beer. They ate a lousy meal and the men in uniform kept glancing furtively at Christa until Ralf eventually took her away. Christa stroked the black, shiny roof of his car and acknowledged his new-found wealth with a little whistle. They leaned against it to kiss and Ralf instantly remembered the taste of her lips. On the way home to Köpenick they spoke in glances. He gripped the steering wheel like a lifebelt.

They got straight into bed, undressing hastily. They made love in silence, under the dome of the duvet, saying very little to each other. She whispered an admission that she had briefly had another boyfriend. He said he had met a woman too, but it meant nothing. He felt her nails digging into his back.

From that day on Christa stayed mostly at Ralf's apartment, even though she had her own. They struck up a close friendship with Krombholz and his wife Mareille. All of them began to make frequent trips together to the North Sea, Ralf taking endless photographs of Christa in the water with his new camera. At the end of each day Ralf and Christa always had each other. It was as though each night she found new ways of sticking her tongue deeper into his mouth.

In October Ralf had to go to Holland. It was the first time in two months that they would be separated for more than a few hours. Just when Ralf could scarcely drag himself away from her, his work was beginning to improve again. He was required to purchase computerized lens-cutting equipment for the Zeiss optics firm. With 70,000 marks in his possession, the responsibility made him almost lightheaded with temptation. But he was not a thief. And it terrified him to think of defecting without Christa.

He promised he would bring her back chocolate, enough to live on for months.

'You just want me to be fat like Mareille Krombholz, isn't that it? You fancy her.'

Ralf laughed. It was a ridiculous suggestion. But a shadow of doubt passed across Christa's face.

'Do you love me?' she asked.

'You know I do, Christa,' he said, kissing her on the top of her head.

She sat on the edge of the bath, swirling her hand in the steaming water. It was just before Ralf left for the train. She became silent as he said goodbye to her. He was dressed and she was naked, holding her wet hands away from him, his buttons cold against her skin, the rough fabric of his coat tickling her nipples.

She looked up into his eyes.

'Ralf, *Schatz*,' she said. 'Are you with the Stasi?'

'Why do you ask that?' he replied instantly. 'I work for the foreign department, Christa. I'd never work with those shits.'

SEVENTEEN

While Ralf was away in Holland, a Stasi member contacted Christa for the first time since she had come to Berlin. Her heart skipped a beat; just when she was beginning to believe they had forgotten about her. A man phoned her at work one morning using the operative name 'Blondi' and refusing to give his own name. But she recognized the persistent tone and the sick Stasi sense of humour; a cross between an undertaker and a chirpy weather forecaster. He simply took it for granted that she would agree to meet him outside Lichtenberg railway station. He said they had a date. He didn't even wait for her to say yes or no.

She stood for twenty minutes in the cold outside the station, silently cursing this Stasi man. She watched people come and go: women with fake fur collars, men in imitation leather coats, any of whom could have been her contact. The whole thing had coincided with a feeling of sickness in her stomach; perhaps she had the flu. She had suffered a peculiar backache over the past few days and began to worry, not so much about the Stasi as about herself. She had been less than cautious. I hope to Jesus I'm not pregnant, she thought.

She was eventually picked up in a black car. The wind caught her dress as she sat in the seat beside a slightly fat, round-faced man wearing a leather jacket over his suit. He wore square glasses with no rims. He was bald and pale and had tufts of hair in his nostrils. He shook hands with her and kept glancing at her knees as he drove to a nearby car park.

'Has Krone got some kind of scrambling equipment in his apartment?'

'I don't know what you mean,' Christa answered.

She felt the blood rushing to her face. The man was suddenly far less pleasant than he had been on the phone. He began to caution her about the consequences of betraying the socialist state. Her brother was not out of trouble yet. She also had her career in Berlin to think about.

'He's got some anti-bugging device set up in his apartment. You'd better start looking for it. It's up to you. You know what you were contracted to do in Leipzig . . .'

He told her not to act so stupid when she said she knew nothing. If she didn't supply them with more information, she would have to find a way of letting them into his apartment quietly.

Christa could smell the man's dumpling breath in the car. He occasionally released a silent burp of air from the side of his mouth. Tapping his pen on a notepad in his lap, he put a string of questions to her about Ralf, and Christa felt a cramping void in her stomach. This was the real conscription, having to get inside her lover's head, confessing what she knew about Ralf to the Stasi. She offered irrelevant information, things about Ralf's dress sense, his manners, his way of walking around the house with his shoelaces undone. There was little else to tell.

'Come on, Blondi. He's been making some funny remarks at the office. What is he thinking? You could help him to get out of trouble.'

What trouble, she asked, but the man avoided the subject and asked her to concentrate on giving him information. She hesitated, and then decided to make thing sound better. She said Ralf Krone loved his work; he had been preparing with some excitement for a conference. That was all she knew. Other than the private details, such as the fact that he was a terrible cook.

'Listen here,' the man said threateningly. His large frame seemed to dominate this brief, frightening conversation. He said

73

he would come back to her again very soon. Looking long and hard at her legs, he advised her to have something decent to talk about the next time. 'It's up to you.'

On the way back to Ralf's apartment she felt depressed. It was all compounded by the fact that Ralf was away and they had pounced when she was alone and most vulnerable. For the first time, she was afraid of the future. Not just of what the Stasi wanted from Ralf but of more personal matters, like pregnancy. Perhaps she would not tell Ralf, just disappear home to Halle for a few days and have a termination.

When Ralf returned, Christa was distant with him. All through dinner she listened to him talking about Holland. She had no appetite. And when they were in bed together she could not hold it back any longer.

'Ralf,' she said, 'this officer came and asked me some questions.'

'Who?'

'Some man, he wouldn't give his name. But he asked me things about you, Ralf, and I didn't know what to say. I told him nothing.'

Ralf cursed them. He sat upright in the bed with his arms folded. Christa wanted to know what Ralf had done and why they were after him.

'It's nothing, *Schatz*. Don't worry about it. It's only routine stuff. You see, I work with a lot of classified documents. They're just obsessed with security.'

Ralf had a way of putting her at ease. He kissed her and stroked her hair. She swore that she would never tell them anything about him anyway.

'I told them you were a lousy cook, that's all,' she said, and they both laughed nervously as though she had inadvertently given away one of their most intimate secrets.

'Just go along with them, sweetheart.'

She felt a little better. She felt she had been honest, even though she could not bring herself to say what was really on her mind, her pregnancy. Ralf rubbed her stomach, accidentally

74

targeting the most sensitive area of her body. And when she began to relax he went under the duvet to kiss her navel, gently pushing her thighs apart with his hands. Christa tried to resist. The lie was in bed with her.

Four days later she felt so ill that she made an appointment with the doctor for a test. It was around the same time that Rainer Krombholz was relocated to the West, to work on a collaborative venture with Western scientists. This brought a further emptiness to their lives. She would miss Mareille, the only person, apart from Ralf, she could talk to.

'We'll never see you any more,' Christa said.

'Don't be crazy,' Krombholz said. 'It gives you both a good reason to come and visit us over there.'

They invited Ralf and Christa to dinner before they left; one last wild evening among friends. There seemed to be a closeness between these four people on that night which had never been so strong before, perhaps only because of the imminent departure of the Krombholzes. Apart from their own love, Ralf and Christa had invested everything in this one friendship. Christa got very drunk. There was a tearful parting, and on the way home she was sick. She was so embarrassed, puking beside the car with Ralf holding her by the shoulders. And afterwards she suddenly felt so depressed that she wanted to spend the night alone in her own apartment. She said she felt trapped and claustrophobic, and when Ralf began to drive again he expressed concern about their relationship.

'You want to leave me?' he said.

'Ralf, you know that's not true,' she said, putting her arm around him. 'I'm just worried. I think I've got the flu. I don't know what's happening to me.'

He stopped the car and they sat for a while in the darkness, their faces illuminated from time to time by passing headlights. There was still a smell of vomit in the air. He wanted to know what worried her, whether it was the Stasi man who had questioned her. She shook her head.

75

'Ralf, I think I'm pregnant,' she admitted finally; the honesty suddenly overwhelmed her and brought her to tears. 'I don't know what to do.'

The temperature in the car had dropped. Steam clouded the windows. She was shivering.

'A baby,' Ralf said. 'That's amazing, Christa.'

He embraced her and began to rub her stomach. He kissed away the tears on her face. He looked at her stomach as though he expected to see some change, reiterating his delight. Now they needed nobody. Now they had a world to themselves. Ralf started the engine and drove her home with reckless speed, glancing at her and smiling all the way.

EIGHTEEN

On the morning of the Stasi conference Ralf was collected in an official black car and driven to Normannen Strasse. He wished it was all over. The occasion evoked no sense of excitement or pride in his achievement but a strong degree of anger at being drawn even further into the state labyrinth. His speech had been vetted. He had been told what to say. Only his preoccupation with Christa and the idea of her having a baby took away from his gloom.

There was frost everywhere that morning. He could see people's breath and the trams chimed in the frozen air. Here and there car drivers rubbed the insides of their windscreens. The parks were lifeless, except for men sweeping and children with large square schoolbags occasionally kicking through the brown heap of leaves. In the schools the maps of Europe placed Moscow at the centre, West Germany on the edge, London up on the outer periphery. Everybody in East Germany knew the Russian words for frost, chestnut leaves, trams and winter. The official communist title for the Christmas angels had been changed to 'winged gift couriers'.

Outside the conference hall the cars were all parked neatly in lines. Some chauffeurs stood around their vehicles stamping their feet. The foyer was much the same as any other MfS interior: the seats were upholstered in blue and the walls were covered with the same blond, ash-veneer panelling as in Ralf's office. Photographers from *Neues Deutschland* were taking pictures but were not permitted beyond the doors of the conference chamber. It was a closed MfS meeting. Ralf was introduced to various senior officers, shaking hands, smiling, occasionally cracking a benign joke in order to take the chill of formality out of the air. He recognized Erich Mielke. Here and there the atmosphere was softened by a waft of perfume. Waiters hurried around with coffee and trays with spiral-patterned poppy-seed cake.

The conference was launched by Mielke, the short, wiry father of state security, who delivered a long opening speech on stability in the national soul. He made security sound like a growth industry, calling for selfless commitment 'in every shoe factory, in every assembly plant, every home, every school . . .'

All morning Ralf listened to one speaker after the other expressing the state paranoia on security. It had nothing to do with the real world, and even though Ralf was a privileged outsider representing the scientific community in the GDR, he realized that he had become a part of the paranoia. One forensic scientist from Leipzig spoke about the setting up of scent banks, an ingenious new method of creating an index of suspects by filing jars of scent swabs. At first there was laughter, followed by hearty clapping originating from where Mielke was sitting.

Ralf opened the afternoon session, delivering his paper energetically, explaining how his science and technology division had provided industries in the East with access to competitive Western ideas. But Ralf's discomfort at taking part in a Stasi conference was eating at him. He saw the complacent faces staring back at him, and impetuously began to depart from his prepared speech.

'What we need is more original ideas,' he said. 'We don't need to copy from the West. We don't need this second-hand culture. Our scientists are not stupid.'

There was no applause. He was taken aback by the silence that reigned in the hall. Already he knew he had said the wrong thing, and as he finished, the Stasi boss took over the podium and changed the subject. Afterwards he was told to report straight to Normannen Strasse headquarters the following day, where Erwin Pückler awaited him, glaring with disgust.

'You have been relieved of your duties,' Pückler said. 'From now on you will be working here with us in headquarters. You will be involved in recruiting unofficial operatives from the academic area.'

'I can't do that. I am a scientist,' Ralf argued weakly.

'You've burned your bridges,' Pückler said furiously. 'Listen, Krone . . . You got us into a lot of shit over what you said. This directive comes straight from Mielke.'

Ralf was given a rundown of his new work practices. For once he was wise enough to keep his mouth shut.

'You'll develop a talent for setting people against each other,' Pückler said. 'After all, security is a science in its own right.'

Ralf thought of escaping to the West. He still had the special travel permit. He wondered whether Christa would go with him. He went to her apartment, and when he saw her, white as a sheet with fear, he knew why.

'They kept me for four hours,' she told him.

'They want me to work with the Stasi now,' he said, switching on the tap in the kitchen.

'I'm going to leave,' he whispered. 'I'm going to the West. Tonight. Let's go, Christa. I'm not going to wait for them to confiscate my travel pass.'

It was the only way out. But Christa was overwhelmed by anxiety, about Thomas and her mother. There seemed no alternative but to come clean with Ralf, and she told him about her contract with the Stasi. She explained how they had forced her to sign on account of her brother. Up until now, she had carefully avoided telling him.

Suddenly Ralf understood everything. 'You agreed to give information about me,' he said accusingly.

'Ralf, you don't understand. I didn't tell them anything. I just signed, that's all. I had to do it for Thomas. Believe me, I never told them anything.'

The tap gushed incessantly, increasing his mistrust. Christa began to cry.

'I'm getting out,' he said. 'Please, Christa, do me this favour at least. Don't squeal on me till I'm out.'

'Ralf, I want to go with you,' Christa said through her tears.

Ralf remained silent. He watched her rubbing the palm of her hand across her eyes and tried to decide what to do, whether he loved her enough. It was as though here, at this moment, they were confronted with a test, a loyalty test which every couple had to undergo sooner or later.

'We'd better get going,' he said eventually, embracing her, and the touch of her body seemed to eliminate all his doubts. Once they were in the West it would all be irrelevant anyway.

He instructed her to pack and wait for him while he drove back to his apartment for the permit. He took only what he could stuff into his coat pockets. When he got back there was a car outside Christa's apartment with two men sitting in it. He decided to risk collecting her. They drove as far as Alexanderplatz where he abandoned the car. It was too predictable to try and escape in a car. They walked across the open space where they had met in the summer. He led her up the steps to the S-Bahn where they waited in the cold, saying nothing. They travelled to Friederich Strasse, the wheels screaming underneath the train like a savage warning. It was dark. They could see the streets below them, headlights of cars stabbing under the bridges.

At the checkpoint, Ralf produced Christa's identity papers.

'I have instructions to bring this young lady to the other side immediately,' he said, handing over his own permit.

'Expulsion?' the guard asked stupidly. He took the documents and turned to walk away towards a glass office.

'These instructions come directly from Mielke,' Ralf said, and the officer hesitated. The name Mielke spread a fallout of respect everywhere. The guard waved them through and Ralf ushered Christa along the corridors to the West side. They did not speak together, unable to grasp the notion of freedom, certain they would be arrested at any moment.

They carried on by U-Bahn, and, though they were technically in the West already, on West Berlin transport, Ralf realized that they still had to pass through more disused East Berlin stations before they were out of GDR territory. It was like a ghost train. Occasionally they saw lights in the tunnels. Sometimes they heard dogs barking. It seemed to take for ever, the train crawling through the jaundiced twilight of GDR stations, border guards with their guns and their muzzled dogs on the platforms. Christa had her hands clasped. The train slowed down almost to a stop. Then it speeded up and, within seconds, rolled eagerly into the first brightly lit West station.

'We're there,' he said.

NINETEEN

Mathias phoned Claudia at work. He was hoping to ask her to help him out with some financial investigations into the Christa Süsskind story, having already prepared to approach her with his request at home the previous evening, but put it off. The fact that he was now in possession of two complimentary tickets for a U2 concert made things much easier. He wanted to hear Claudia's little squeal of delight; she couldn't get enough of U2 and usually reverted to a mindless teenager at the mere mention of tickets.

She wasn't in the office, however, when he phoned. He made nothing of it at first, but when he phoned back an hour later and she was still out, he became suspicious. Not for the first time, he felt he was policing her movements. She had become quite obsessed with Ireland, frequently going back to the Oscar Wilde pub with Alexandra, taking out Irish movies on video, even getting people at the Irish bar to write out the words of her favourite ballads. Not only that, she had also become more distant and tended to lie awake at night, dreaming about the Atlantic.

What Mathias didn't know was that she was out having lunch with Kevin at the time. Their intial physical attraction had developed into quite an attachment. It was perfectly innocent, she told herself. She had simply discovered a sense of fun about him that seemed to have gone missing from her own life of late.

When he quietly asked her out to lunch, it seemed like the most natural progression. She turned it down, of course. But when he asked her again, putting it to her as though everyone else was going as well, she reconsidered. Initially, she thought Alexandra would join them, and accepted, fully intending to tell Mathias about it. Then she realized that Alexandra couldn't make it. Even as Kevin began to suggest the names of restaurants, Claudia had subconsciously begun to map out a kind of territory of engagement by turning down locations which she and Mathias had already been to. It was not meant to lead to anything. It was purely imaginary.

Kevin gave her his number at work, just in case something came up. And Claudia had found herself going home with Kevin's number on a beermat in her bag, memorized it instead, and threw the beermat out of the car window, almost like a murder weapon. When she met Kevin two days later for lunch, she was a little nervous. Luckily, he kept talking all the time about home, and it was only towards the end, when he had paid the bill and walked her back to her car, that she began to relax and feel the thrill of the meeting. Other than the parting handshake, which he may have held on to for a little too long, Kevin had not forced himself or suggested another meeting. It was just lunch, she was able to convince herself. Nothing more.

She phoned Mathias back at 3 that afternoon, angry because he had phoned three times. 'You shouldn't keep ringing like that, Matt.' She explained that she had been out shopping with Alexandra and it could be embarrassing because she had come back late.

Mathias concealed his suspicions. He mentioned the U2 tickets and heard the tiny squeal of acknowledgment, though he had expected a more energetic barrage of superlatives. She used the commercial term '*super*', pronounced with loud ascending Z. She also employed the more established word '*klasse*', and rushed into endearing phrases borrowed from pop music. 'I love you, Matt,' she said in English, but it sounded false, like somebody on MTV. Maybe all Germans had temporarily run out of superlatives.

'Claudia, can I ask you to do something for me?' Mathias said.

Claudia had already anticipated some kind of reciprocal catch. Because of her job at American Express, he had once or twice before persuaded her to run a microscopic credit check through Germany's financial institutions on certain people. She was far more competent at this than anyone he knew in the financial section of the *Tageszeitung*. Now he wanted her to check out the names of Erwin Pückler and Rainer Krombholz. So far he had come up with nothing but blanks and his efforts on the Christa Süsskind story had been spectacularly unsuccessful.

Claudia jotted down the names. As an afterthought, Mathias also gave her the name of Ralf Krone, just in case. He explained in a few words that this was very important; he was pursuing the case of an East German woman involved in forced adoption. Claudia became curious. A moment ago she couldn't wait to get off the phone, but then she was hit by an absurd interest and began asking Mathias for the woman's name and where she was from. She wanted to know the whole circumstances. She even asked about the woman's present marital status.

'Claudia, I can tell you more about it at home,' Mathias said.

'I've got time now. I'd like to know.'

Mathias hastily sketched a dispassionate outline of Christa's past. But explaining the details to Claudia over the phone like this seemed to cast everything in a fog of suspicion, as though his sudden obsession in East Germany's past looked like an unhealthy male perversion.

'Why former East Germany?' she asked.

Mathias told her he was on to a big story. But Claudia wasn't convinced. She kept wanting to know more about Christa Süsskind, where she was living now and, even more absurd, what age she was. Her guilt at having lunch with Kevin had made her completely irrational.

'Look, Claudia. There's nothing in it. I'm just doing a story, that's all.'

'I'm only asking, Matt.'

But there was a subtle, underlying entrenchment. Mathias had harassed the *Tageszeitung* rock critic for the U2 tickets in order to reduce all of this complacent matrimonial distance between himself and Claudia of late. Their dialogue seemed to stumble more and more along beaten paths into domestic jargon, and old battle formations. Their subject matter consisted merely of family timetables, new curtains, repairing the perimeter fence in the garden, the idea of getting a boat for the lake: all the usual family ambitions and all the usual crises acted out like pre-ordained plots. Even the tickets were a practicality, rather than a gesture of affection. They had become mutually suspicious of one another. Was it Mathias's indiscretions in the past? Was it Claudia's new attachment to Kevin? Was it the inability to pool their aspirations as they had always done before? Something which prevented them from undertaking anything together, as though the former intensity of their love had now gone below a critical marker that began to turn it to hatred and jealousy and all the deeply trying irritations inflicted on people sharing the same space.

Their time together was increasingly taken up by little conquests over equality, often reaching a ridiculous level of banality. It mattered who had seen what new movie first. Or who had read which book first. Their relationship thrived on minor contests over who was having the best time. Sometimes they talked about their problems together, holding official healing discussions in order to understand each other. Maturity had brought this compulsion to explain rather than experience anything together. As though fun had been replaced by science and analysis. Mathias explained that he was in the grip of a career obsession, hoping to move up a step or two. He had asked Claudia to understand his need to work hard, to build for the future. For two weekends in a row Claudia and Werner had gone to the garden without him. Mathias and Claudia were going in opposite directions.

Of course, they had sex. They were always coming from or going towards the next orgasm. In fact the regularity and perfection of their lovemaking was breathtaking. But pleasure was always covered over by a blanket of sleep and forgetting. Occasionally it went beyond anything they had achieved before and became unforgettable, like the time by the lake at night, with a full moon, in the middle of winter after the Van Morrison concert. Or the night after the last party. But the words they exchanged afterwards always seemed ironically like nature's way of reducing the burden of intimacy. Nature's way of restoring an acceptable distance. Were they unable to be close? Had they arrived at some protocol which made love impossible?

TWENTY

There was a small wooden jetty not far from the allotment where they put the new canoe into the water. Mathias and Werner were able to carry it down alone before lunch, it was so light, even though they were both barefoot and had to walk carefully, suffering the small pebbles on the path. Werner was already wearing the bright green lifejacket and his long patterned swimming trunks underneath.

Mathias put the paddles together while Werner stepped into the canoe, wobbling at first as he held on to the jetty. Mathias talked to him a little about how far out on to the lake he could go; he had to avoid the yachts and, above all, the swimmers. There were few swimmers around at the time, but he had to be careful; you didn't want to knock some woman's teeth out in the water. Werner listened as though all of this were superfluous talk. He had canoed before with friends and took off like a shot.

Mathias dived into the water after him, still calling out instructions, trying to catch up as Werner paddled swiftly in wide circles. The sound of their voices carried across the surface of the water, and for Werner there was something warm and eternally safe about the way the sun shone down on his father's head below him. For twenty minutes they raced each other back and forth, Werner giving Mathias a head start each time.

After lunch, Mathias took a turn at the canoe himself. He had trouble with instability while he was getting his legs into the hold, but then he paddled around quite confidently. He had never been in a canoe before and was, in some ways, far more excited about

87

it than his son was. He often wondered whether kids today were capable of showing joy as he used to. He felt Werner sometimes just soaked things up without any reaction, responding with grown-up erudition as though he'd seen everything. Werner's emotions seemed to be controlled by commerce and it was uncool to acknowledge any form of instinctive gladness other than the minimal response such as 'not bad' or 'wow' or simply 'thanks, Dad'. The world he was growing up in allowed no room for surprise or primitive expressions of happiness.

When Claudia arrived at the jetty with Alexandra and Klaus and Kevin, she began to laugh at Mathias from the shore. Her derision was perhaps a sign that she still related to her family and had not yet broken away.

'Reverting to boyhood,' she muttered, and then, shouting across the water, 'You're such a natural, Matt.'

'Deliverance,' somebody remarked.

'Do an Eskimo roll.'

Staring into the sunlight, Mathias could just about recognize Claudia in her one-piece dark green swimsuit, with Werner by her side. He paddled towards the jetty, taking care not to threaten the swimmers who had begun to take over the water. Alexandra dived into the lake followed by Kevin. Over lunch they had all talked about Ireland again, Claudia leading the discussion with her favourite bits from the *Commitments* film.

When Alexandra met the canoe in the water, she held on to the bow and called out to Kevin to come and tip the boat over. But Mathias voluntarily disembarked, awkwardly pulling his legs out after him, enjoying the sudden muffled quality of voices as his head went under water. He saw Alexandra's legs kicking and swam underneath her to pull her down by the waist. Her amplified scream was cut short by the immersion.

The rest of the afternoon was given over to everyone else taking turns in the canoe. Kevin and Klaus were clearly the most practised, speeding out into the lake by turn, adeptly spinning the boat around in circles.

'There's nothing to it,' Klaus called back towards the jetty, trying to encourage the women to go next.

'You won't find me in that thing,' Claudia said. Everything she said seemed to echo the spiritual dilemma on the threshold of an affair.

She sat on the edge of the jetty, legs dangling, painted toenails occasionally dipping into the water. She wanted to try but felt she needed more encouragement. She was aware that Kevin was watching her all the time. Alexandra turned out to be even better than Klaus. She displayed a real talent for paddles and Klaus was chuffed at her late conversion to sport.

'No way,' Claudia kept saying when it came to her turn, and Mathias thought it was odd that Kevin should join in, trying to encourage her.

On the surface Claudia ignored Kevin. But she enjoyed having all of them urging her to get into the boat. It appealed to her individuality, her sense of being a woman rather than a wife, or a mother, or any of the other categories imposed on her by life in Berlin. But it was for Werner that she agreed to have a go at the canoe in the end, feeling that she was undertaking something morally dangerous, something irrevocable.

'I'm terrified,' she admitted openly, holding on to Mathias around the waist. 'Save your mother,' she called out to Werner with exaggerated angst as she lowered her feet down. Getting into the canoe was an ordeal. She was unsure and felt quite vulnerable. The striped marks of the jetty planks were imprinted on the back of her legs. She gripped Mathias's ankle. Kevin kept watching her stomach move in and out with her breathing as she tried to steady herself. The way the boat shimmied under her feet made her giggle nervously, and it was only Alexandra's contagious laughter that made everything seem funny instead of disastrous.

'Let me out,' Claudia shouted, glancing over at the sunbathers on the shore close by. But she already felt better about the whole thing as she sat down into the canoe. It was Klaus who pushed her off and tried to instruct her from the jetty, though his words had no effect because she found it impossible to distinguish between the function of right and left. The fact that she could not stop laughing didn't help. It made her weak. With each paddle she seemed to go around in a circle, making only lateral progress if any, away from the jetty. Every now and again a sudden movement would make her stop laughing and squint back at her audience.

'You should see her driving the car,' Mathias muttered.

'Oh now, that's a bit low,' Alexandra said, slapping him on the arm.

'She's had too much wine.'

'Not true,' Alexandra defended. 'Claudia, you're doing fine. *Spitze!*'

Claudia got the hang of it, finally. As she paddled out, it all seemed so much easier than she had anticipated. Before anyone realized it, she began to impress them with a sudden burst of speed. On the way back towards the shore, though, it became clear to her and everyone else that she was heading straight for one of the bathers. She had no way of stopping herself. Having gathered quite a bit of momentum, she was about to steer right into his bobbing, bald head. Both Klaus and Mathias began to call out urgent instructions. The swimmer tried to swim clear, but each time Claudia's efforts to avoid him succeeded only in pointing the canoe more directly at him.

'Oh my God,' Alexandra said, giggling and holding her hand up to her mouth.

'Paddle backwards,' Klaus shouted.

'With the left side,' Mathias echoed.

Claudia could do nothing to stop herself. She closed her eyes and sailed on. Werner turned his back. Mathias began to whistle. It was Klaus who shouted, '*Achtung!*' and the swimmer put up his hand up to deflect the course of the canoe with a small, neat push at the bow.

TWENTY-ONE

Claudia's affair began one Thursday evening after work. She was surprised at how soon the relationship developed into a sexual one. Immediately, almost. After their Italian meal, Kevin had casually come up with a list of places they could go for a drink. Finally, he'd said, there was always the Irish pub, or his own apartment. His colleague was away in Dresden at the time. It seemed perfectly logical that they should choose his apartment. She just smiled, and it was only at that moment that she became aware of what she was doing, not as a crime but as a fantasy which had taken on real life. With it came a wild sensation of excitement which almost made her weak. It felt like being involved in a plane crash, or some extraordinary event which made everything unreal; her life cast on a screen in an American film. She was lightheaded with love. She was surprised that she didn't stop herself; all that scrupulous self-analysis seemed to disappear.

On the first night she even became practical, calmly putting down all kinds of rules which would belong to their affair. She called them the 'Oscar Wilde' rules, after the Irish bar where they would have to practise maximum discretion in case Mathias should go there. Kevin was never to phone her at home. He was not to try and speak to her, or stare at her, if they met in the company of her husband. There were to be no surprises; he was not to do anything without asking her first. There would be no display of affection in public and they would speak English at all times, ensuring that the relationship was always conducted in a semi-imaginary, foreign land; a territory which would never overlap that of her family. They would behave as though they were on holiday in Ireland.

Their conversation was sometimes limited to macaronic peculiarities, often revolving around syntax and her occasional mispronunciation of the letter W. They would both laugh when Kevin imitated the havoc played by German sentence construction on English sentences, like, 'We will meet us on Thursday.' She could see how this kind of fun would eventually become unbearably trite. She could even imagine losing all affection for Irish songs, once the novelty wore off. She could see that Kevin was not exactly handsome either, and that if she allowed herself to make a comparison between him and Mathias on any level, physical or intellectual, it might all fall apart instantly. But she had become blind to logic. And for the time being their meetings were driven by real inspiration.

There were moments on the first evening when she might have stopped herself and called it off. At the door of Kevin's apartment she felt that rush of intense excitement which seemed to hit her like a fever; too much alcohol, or too much coffee. Her clothes, her underwear, everything seemed to have been prepared for this. It was premeditated. A fleeting image of Mathias came to her and she suddenly remembered the exact sound of the way he said, 'For God's sake, Claudia.' But she ignored this and rushed ahead, kissing Kevin's face as though any delay might bring back the obstacles of her own sexual superstitions and reduce this invented intimacy to nothing. At her request, Kevin sang as she undressed. It took her attention away from the awkwardness of being naked in front of him, lying back on the bed. It was so unlike being naked on the beach, and so unlike that parallel moment at home with Mathias, which had become surrounded by a strict code of tact. At home she had to reconstruct mystery all the time. Here with Kevin she was empowered by an endless supply, as long as she didn't stop to think too much, and as long as Kevin kept singing or making love. He had a particularly charming way of repeating the word 'Lovely, lovely, lovely.' She was flattered by his attention to detail.

In the following days Claudia felt alive and independent on the one hand, weak and deceitful on the other. The affair with Kevin had restored a huge sexual power and a feeling of danger and adventure which she had forgotten about. She found herself initiating everything.

At home, it was all friction and boredom. She kept saying she was ill and refused Mathias quite indelicately one night when he suddenly began to kiss her stomach. 'Not like that,' she said, shifting the blame on to his clumsiness rather than her unwillingness. That came on the night she told him she had found out nothing about the Christa Süsskind case except for the fact that Krombholz had a bank account in West Berlin up until 1989.

Hurt by her rejection, Mathias kept making greater efforts at home. He phoned her at work. And eventually he formed very real suspicions when she had gone sick at work and he could not find her anywhere, neither at home nor at the doctor. He soon found himself persecuted by his own imagination. His suspicions fell on Klaus first. But he felt he could not confront Claudia yet because she would fly into a rage and accuse him of behaving like an old Stasi. Their relationship could not survive another war. Even Werner was beginning to notice the strain and kept to himself in his own room.

The conversation Mathias should have had with Claudia was eventually conducted with Klaus instead. He dropped over to his apartment, if only to speak openly to a friend.

'Klaus, I think Claudia is fooling around,' he said, looking at Klaus's eyes for an immediate reaction.

'How do you know that?'

'I just have this feeling. You kind of know when something is happening. She's been missing from work. Says she's been out with Alexandra, shopping.'

'Shit,' Klaus said. 'I'd never have thought it, Matt. Honestly.'

'You know, if there is something going on, I'd just like to know, that's all. I don't want to be this fucking idiot in the background.'

The fact that Klaus did nothing to reject the veiled accusation, seemed to put him temporarily beyond any culpability.

'I don't know who to suspect even,' Klaus said. 'Somebody at the office?'

They talked for a while, exchanged a few names and drank beer. When Alexandra came back she said she found it all impossible to believe.

'Claudia?' she said. 'You must be joking. You think I wouldn't know?'

'Then why do I feel so uneasy?'

'Matt, what is wrong with you? I think you're making this up. Have you asked her about it?'

'No. Not yet.'

TWENTY-TWO

On the day of the U2 concert, Claudia phoned Mathias at work in the afternoon to say she couldn't go. He was mystified. Developing another acute migraine attack just hours before a live performance of her favourite band was as close as Claudia could get to admitting that something was going on.

'Claudia, I don't understand this,' he said. 'You said you'd rather die than miss this concert.'

'Don't rub it in, Matt. Don't you think I know what I'm missing? I just couldn't take all that noise tonight.'

'*Noise?* I can't believe I'm hearing this. Claudia, are you fooling around or something? If you are, I'd like to know.'

'Jesus,' she said, seething with anger. 'What the hell . . .? I'm not even going to answer that, Matt. How dare you?' Then she just put down the phone.

Claudia was not to be cured. No amount of Tylenol would make her go to U2 with him that night. Mathias thought of selling the tickets. Then he thought of pretending to go to the concert and returning to see what Claudia was really up to. It tormented him to think that she was basically refusing his company. He had hoped the concert would somehow repair the fracture which had developed between them. It seemed she still agreed to make love occasionally, but drew the line at the spiritual intimacy of a U2 concert; as though she could not submit to the emotional fervour, getting excited and screaming like a teenager in his presence. She was up to something.

'You'll be sorry,' Mathias said, trying to make light of it

when they met at home later. 'You're not a real fan.'

'Mathias, don't be a bastard. You've said enough already to hurt me.'

Mathias ended up taking Werner with him, even though he was a little too young and made Mathias feel a little too old. Werner was thrilled. They sat in the special seating area and Mathias derived, instead, a father's pleasure of explaining things to his son. They watched the daylight fading and the moon rising. A breeze blew over the audience below them like a surging sea of heads and raised arms. Over the roar of the crowd they could occasionally identify an individual whistle or shout. Fans around them were already singing the words. The spotlights came on, the screens were being tested, and in a way Mathias was reminded of going to Mass as a child – candles being lit, the feeling of awe and respect for something larger and stronger and more fulfilling than the mundane world. The band arrived on stage with a rush of sound and random images on the screens. The energy of the audience snapped into a frenzy.

While it was possible to talk without shouting into each other's ears Werner kept remarking about things. He didn't understand everything. Nor did Mathias. It all seemed more like one continuous spiritual climax in which the crowd played a much more important role than the band: this conspiracy among thousands of people to believe in the same thing. It was the crowd that breathed life into the event. Mass culture had not changed in a thousand years.

Mathias found that he had completely forgotten about Claudia. He felt relieved by her denial and dismissed her betrayal as fantasy. Maybe he had begun to succumb to the frantic and benign pulse of the crowd. The three Trabis were hoisted up over the stage on wires and Mathias suddenly began to think back to East Germany under communism. How would they have felt if they had imagined their sawdust and fibreglass vehicle becoming a piece of living rock culture? The Trabi, their museum-piece of industrial failure and noxious fumes, sucked forward into a new tyranny of fun and entertainment?

On the way out from the concert there was a tight crush where the crowd funnelled out through the exits and Mathias held Werner in front of him. They were breathing the collective heat, sweat and hair shampoo of the crowd. Some made humorous remarks about the crush while others whispered ecstatic praise of the event. Mostly everyone endured the silent squeeze of bodies, still shocked by the energy and the assault of sound still buzzing in their ears. Pushed up beside Werner was a young girl of around sixteen or seventeen who smiled down at him and then glanced back to see the boy's father. Mathias only saw her face and her smile for one instant. He was left looking at the back of her head and her long hair.

Outside the gates, where the crowd exploded into the greater freedom of the street, Mathias brushed accidentally against the girl's arm. She didn't notice it. Only Mathias became aware that the back of his hand and forearm had skimmed by her upper arm with an electric sensation of softness. It was what they talked about in TV ads. To him it was as though he had never felt skin like it before; it was so inadvertently erotic. And walking ahead with one hand on Werner's shoulder, he could not resist looking back to get a look at the young woman's face again.

At home Claudia was already asleep, but as he got into bed he wanted to find out if her skin was as soft; whether there was a comparison to be made. Could the brush with the girl outside the stadium possibly have been an illusion? He stroked his forearm lightly against Claudia's bare upper arm. He did it three times, just to be sure, almost waking her up. Perhaps he had never consciously done anything like this before, without Claudia's knowledge. He was amazed. The softness was identical. It was extraordinary, he thought, even if this scientific test didn't quite match up to the erotic clash after the concert. It was as though he didn't know her.

TWENTY-THREE

After the escape to the West, Christa and Ralf had no idea where to go. They drifted along on the U-Bahn, unable to believe their own luck, hugging each other occasionally when there was nobody looking. Eventually they surfaced at Kurfürsten Strasse station and walked along Potsdamer Strasse linking arms. The night was cold and they stood looking into the shop windows, their faces lit up by the glow of neon. They had never been so much alone together before.

At an open-air fast-food stand Christa became hypnotized by the rotating cone of kebab meat. The exotic smells acted on her like a narcotic as she watched the Turk behind the counter slapping lettuce, cabbage, meat and sauce together; a sacred rite of the free world. Unwittingly attracting the attention of a drunk clinging to one of the high tables, wheeling around with a can of Bitburger in his hand, they moved on to a bar on the other side of Potsdamer Strasse.

Later, when it came to paying for their drinks, Ralf searched through his pockets in a hot panic. 'I was sure I had more than that,' he said, counting his way like a child through grubby notes and coins, calculating what he had already spent at the food stand. Christa started giggling. It was the sudden warmth, the beer, the kebab; the dreamy oblivion of pregnancy.

'Come on, Christa, this is serious,' Ralf said. 'We've nowhere to go. We've no money.'

They discussed their options. They would present themselves

to the West authorities in the morning. Perhaps they should find a youth hostel.

'What about Krombholz?' Christa asked. 'You still have his address, don't you?'

'He's Stasi, Christa. We couldn't go to him.'

'Of course we could. They're our friends. We need someone we can trust. We'll just stay with them one night, until we get sorted out. Besides, what can they do to us now?'

Ralf dug out the address, in Neuköln. He was reluctant to go straight there and decided to phone Krombholz first, to see how he reacted. But he said nothing about their defection and Krombholz agreed to meet them at an Italian restaurant nearby. Since Mareille wasn't there, they would have to eat out. Ralf tried to tell him that they had already eaten a kebab but Krombholz wouldn't listen. Their arrival had provided him with an excuse to eat.

At the restaurant Ralf announced that Christa was pregnant. Dramatic as always, Krombholz got up from his seat and went round to Christa to congratulate her, picking up her hand from the table and kissing it lightly with his big cherub lips.

'Come on, Rainer,' Christa said, smiling. 'It's been known to happen before, you know.'

'I know, but not for us,' Krombholz said and sat down again. 'I'm delighted for you both. Wait till Mareille hears about this.'

The waiter came to take the order. Christa and Ralf said they would share a pizza between them.

'Really, folks, you should give me some notice next time,' Krombholz said. 'How long have you got?'

'Actually, that's something I've got to tell you, Rainer,' Ralf said quietly, glancing at Christa. 'We're here for good. You see, we've had some trouble with the MfS.'

'Shit,' Krombholz said.

'We slipped across this evening.'

'Ralf, you can't do this to me,' Krombholz said, looking around nervously at the other guests in the restaurant. His mood changed completely. 'You defect and you come straight to me,' he whispered angrily. 'They're probably watching me, Ralf, did you think of that? I'll be hanged for this.'

There was silence as they ate the pizza, Christa staring at the food as though it were a painting, too precious to eat. Krombholz wanted to know what he had said at the conference and Ralf explained.

'That was really smart, all right . . . Why does every half-decent scientist want to throw himself on his own sword, can you explain that? Scientists and sports stars, you're all the same.'

Krombholz wiped his forehead with a green paper napkin. He leaned forward, looked at them earnestly and advised them to get out of West Berlin immediately. The Stasi would come looking for them. Ralf was sitting on too much information and they had liquidated other Stasi defectors in the past.

'We're thinking of going to Holland,' Ralf said. 'But we've no money.'

'Holland is not far enough if you ask me.'

Krombholz agreed to take them to the youth hostel. He promised to help them. He calculated how much they would get on the sale of Ralf's camera, how much they would receive from the West authorities and how much they would still need for their airfare to Frankfurt or Munich. Krombholz agreed to lend them the balance on the strict condition that they would give it back once they got settled down.

'Some magazine money maybe?' Ralf said.

Krombholz laughed nervously. He drove them to the youth hostel and Ralf began to regret that he had made contact with him. The terror of their recent escape played back over his mind. He could hardly sit still in the car. Krombholz began to talk of a cousin with a high post at the University of Vienna. Perhaps there was a chance Ralf could get in there. He would look into it. He pulled up outside the hostel and they parted quickly, agreeing to meet the following day at the café on Potsdamer Strasse.

They got a room together at the hostel. Christa sat down heavily on one of the beds, exhausted, and Ralf looked out of the window over the city at the tiny figures shuffling along pavements below, bathed in the pink of neon lights. Christa sat with her arms folded, trying to hold on to a diminishing sense of place in her life. He came over and sat beside her on the bed, embracing her. They made love. There were no curtains and the lights of the city illuminated their bodies. They were plunged into a spirit of affluence, into a reckless love which brought them as close to freedom as they would ever get.

TWENTY-FOUR

In the morning, Ralf sold his camera. It gave them something to live on for a few days as well as contributing to the airfare. Ralf intended to be frugal but was deflected by Christa's new fixation for cakes. Every 200 metres she wanted to stop at a café. And it took her ages to make each excruciating choice. Every cake was like buying a new car. By noon they were wandering through the large shops around Taunzienstrasse.

It was their first day of freedom in the West and Christa soon developed a backache from walking so much. She loved the escalators, and would lean on the side rail to alleviate the pressure around the base of her spine. Whenever she sat down she would feel the full, delicious reversal of pain.

Ralf went to meet Krombholz on his own. Krombholz had been unable to get the entire sum of money together, and they had to wait until Monday. He said he had phoned Vienna and was certain to arrange something there. Ralf became engrossed with the idea of going back to his academic career. He took the warnings from Krombholz seriously, about how they dealt with Stasi defectors. He went to the Staatsbibliothek to do some research, vowing to pursue a brilliant career.

Christa kept going through the shops, and when she came back in the afternoon she found Ralf dozing on the bunk in the small room. She produced a large Ke De We bag full of goods and Ralf sat up, astonished.

'Where the hell did you get all these things?' he demanded.

Christa ignored him, pulling out lingerie, blouses, tights and dresses from the bag.

'Here, I've got something for you, Ralf,' she said, producing several pairs of men's socks.

'Christa, this is not funny,' he said. 'You'll get us arrested.'

'You need socks, Ralf,' she said.

Ralf took the bag off her and dug out the rest of the items – perfume bottles, skin cream, soap, about six different brands of lipstick, combs, brushes, hair removers; every conceivable beauty aid. There was enough underwear for ten women. 'For fuck's sake, Christa,' he exclaimed. Then he pulled out two watches and threw everything on to the bed.

Christa shrugged. She said she had expected him to be grateful, not to get so caught up in his high morals. But it wasn't a moral question, Ralf argued. He couldn't care less what she took. What concerned him was purely the risk of getting caught.

'Do you not want me to wear these things?' she said bitterly, picking up the items one by one.

'It's not that, Christa,' he said. 'I just didn't think you would be so fucking stupid. We can't afford to get caught.'

'What's so stupid about this?' she said angrily, holding up a pair of red satin briefs. One by one she held things out towards him. She began to throw herself into provocative poses, holding an ornate black bra up to her bosom, turning around to push her bottom out towards him.

'You don't appreciate me,' she accused him.

He looked away, and when she persisted, defiling her face with crooked lines of wine-red lipstick that wildly distorted her looks, he stood up and shouted, 'Give it up, Christa.'

His voice echoed around the small, faceless hostel room. She began to cry and he stepped over to comfort her.

That evening she dressed up in all her new clothes and put on far too much make-up. Ralf suggested that women in the West didn't use lipstick as rouge on their cheeks any more. He said only Polish women did that.

On the Sunday they went for a walk in the Tiergarten. It was warm enough in the sunshine to sit on a bench. They listened to two old women talking, one of them holding a lead with a small dog which occasionally growled at the sight of other passing dogs. Now behave yourself, my little bunny rabbit, they heard the woman say. But why did the woman not get herself a rabbit in that case, Ralf asked, and Christa laughed. Once the women had gone she lay down on the bench with her head on his lap.

They met Krombholz again on Monday. Mareille was ecstatic, embracing Christa, touching her tummy.

'*Mein Gott, Schätzen*, a little baby,' she kept saying.

Krombholz had set Ralf up with a great contact in Vienna, he said. He planned everything out for them, suggesting they first go to Munich, where they could stay with friends before going on by car to Vienna.

It was late in the day, some two weeks after their escape to the West, that they set off from Munich towards Vienna. Along with the flight to Munich, Krombholz had arranged accommodation and a driver who would take them all the way, an old friend named Herbert Eisenbein. They drove all afternoon along the Autobahn, past Berchtesgaden up to Salzburg. By the time they were halfway, it was night, and Herbert said he had to drop something off with a relative near Linz.

They drove off the Autobahn for a while into some woods. Ralf became suspicious and asked where they were going, but got no answer. A few hundred metres on they came to a stop near a quarry, with a wall of rock in front of them. Ralf looked out. They were surrounded by men. He was pulled from the car and beaten over the head with a truncheon. He struggled, but was dragged to a nearby workman's hut. It felt as though his head had been opened up, cold air rushing inside.

Christa screamed. She got out and ran after Ralf, shouting, 'My husband, my husband.' She felt a fist crack against the side of her face, and she was sure her jaw was broken. She screamed again. But they were in a deserted place. All she could see was the cold stone face of the quarry in the headlights. Everywhere was so quiet. Another fist caught her full on her mouth, cutting her teeth right into her lip. A hand in a glove covered her mouth and she tasted the sweet terror of her own blood. Somebody punched her violently in the stomach, and she folded over as they pushed her into the back of a van. She was sick, all over her clothes.

Ralf tripped and fell in the workman's hut. He heard Christa shouting outside, but it was dark and he could see nothing. He was kicked in the chest and stomach. His hands went to shield his groin, then his face, then his groin again, protecting neither. The boots were coming from everywhere, hundreds of them it seemed. Through the numb incapacity of fear, he began to realize how badly he had been cheated. A boot connected with the side of his head and everything went black.

TWENTY-FIVE

Ralf awoke in a small cell and saw daylight coming in through a high prison window. Everything had been taken from him – his belt, his scarf, shoelaces. He looked around and saw an enamel mug of malt coffee along with a slice of bread on the floor beside him. He could not eat. He could hardly even drink the lukewarm liquid. His tongue was swollen and he found one of his molar teeth missing, a taste of blood and gum in its place. There was dried blood on his chin and on the wooden bunk where his head had lain. One eye was almost completely closed and there was a constant pain in his ear.

When the guard came to take away the mug and plate, Ralf knew from the uniform that he was in Prague. He had been taken across the Czech border. He cursed Krombholz. It had all been planned: the flight to Munich, the lift to Vienna, all paid for and arranged by the MfS. The chronology of the past few weeks haunted him.

The guard outside kept looking into the cell every five minutes. During the lonely hours of that first day in this Czech detention cell, Ralf tried to discipline himself. He knew he could not allow his mind to stray. He measured the cell, two metres across and three metres long. Nobody spoke to him. The guard gave him soup through the hatch at midday. Later he was taken out to wash and the water ran red. Back in his cell he fluctuated between fury and self-pity, and at one point became hysterical, banging on the door with his fist, but nobody came and he realized that these outbursts would ultimately inflict damage only on himself.

Towards evening, when the light outside faded, his physical pain began to diminish. But the luxury of this slow healing brought back more clearly the reality of the world from which he had been plucked: the lights of West Berlin and Munich; the smell of the underground, the taste of beer and wurst. He could not sleep. He thought only of Christa, remembering her as she was at the beginning, in Leipzig, and when she first came to Berlin. The images transported him away from the prison; his imagination at least was still free.

The following morning, after the malt coffee and bread, the door of his cell was unlocked and opened. There stood Erwin Pückler, smiling.

'Ah, Herr Doktor Krone. Had a nice holiday, then?'

Ralf said nothing, sitting on his bunk, defiantly staring at the face which had already become the object of his entire hatred. He despised Pückler's glasses, and the smug way in which he joked about Ralf's misfortune. Refusing to speak was Ralf's only way of showing resistance. Pückler even showed pleasure at this defiance, calmly removing his glasses and cleaning them with a handkerchief from his pocket. There were two red dimples left behind by the glasses on the bridge of his nose. Pückler behaved wearily, as though he had travelled all night to see Ralf.

'You won't be sending any more fucking postcards, *mein Freund*,' he said leaning into the cell and smiling at the poetic crispness of his own words.

During the day Ralf was transported back to Hohenschönhausen prison in Berlin. It was dark as he arrived and the guards issued instructions in German. He was not permitted to talk, or sing. While sleeping he had to keep his hands out over the blankets. During the day he was not permitted to lie down with or without the blankets. Writing on the walls was forbidden. It sounded like the terms and conditions for a long stay. There was a bucket in the corner. The light behind the grid above the door stayed on, and all night people came to look in at him.

The full shock of captivity only began to grind its way into his intellect after a few days in Hohenschönhausen. He noticed the dogs barking. And the cold. Again and again he felt the black radiator for heat which did not exist. He spent four days and nights in complete isolation before anyone communicated with him. That was the worst part, not talking, as though all his talents were wasted in this cell. He began to argue with himself, sensing the danger of his own madness. He made attempts to contact people in other cells, tapping on the walls, on the pipes, on the floor, waiting each time, hallucinating a faint echo through the concrete. Occasionally he heard a door banging and his entire soul fled towards it.

On the fifth day he was brought for interrogation. His bruises had gone almost black along his chest and arms. It was a luxury to hear the voice of a guard shouting at him, as though at last he could extract some meaning from his surroundings. He noticed the red light at the end of each corridor. He thought he understood the geography of the building. For some reason he had assumed he was on the first or second floor and he laughed at the fact that he had tried for days to make contact with imaginary inmates beneath him.

He was taken up a flight of stairs and led into a room on the first floor. Behind a desk sat Pückler and two other officers.

'Welcome to Hohenschönhausen,' Pückler grinned.

He was questioned on his time in the West. Every detail of the two weeks was recorded. He was asked about Christa, about their plans and who they had met in the West.

'It could make a difference to the magistrate if you co-operated, Herr Doktor.'

But Ralf remained defiant, giving only a minimal account of himself. Pückler leaned back, and the deliberate delay emphasized the pleasure with which he conducted this interview. He scratched his neck with a pencil. Then he began to shout, filling the whole room with his high-pitched voice.

'I want to know what you did with the money.'

'What money?' Ralf asked.

'The money for the Zeiss cutting machine.'

'I gave it to the firm in Holland. We got the delivery, you know that,' Ralf said.

'You have it stuck in a nice fat little bank account somewhere.'

Pückler gave the impression that Ralf could still redeem himself if he co-operated. But when Ralf ignored him, Pückler came over and gave him a blow to his left ear, sending a spasm of pain shooting through his head. Afterwards he apologized and said they were all intelligent people. Pückler realized that he could do far more damage to Ralf by tormenting him with talk of Christa.

'You will never see her again,' he said. 'For you, it's over with Blondi. That will be somebody else's pleasure from now on.'

This interrogation was repeated every day almost word for word, Pückler taunting him with the choice between execution and life imprisonment. At times he resorted to lewd images of Christa. 'You'd love to get a hold of her again, wouldn't you? Well, I'm sorry, Krone, that juicy little cat will belong to somebody else now.'

Ralf tried to contain his anger. The interrogation went on for six days. Sometimes Pückler spoke to Ralf in a friendly manner.

'It beats me how you could have thrown away such a wonderful opportunity. You had everything – a great job, a car, a luxury flat, one of the most beautiful little girls in our state.'

'Where is she?' Ralf asked finally, abandoning all caution.

Pückler beamed at his desperation. 'Right now that little bitch is upstairs with one of the guards,' he said. 'Listen. Can't you hear the springs rocking?'

Ralf leaped from his chair, but the guards caught him immediately. In his rage he began to curse Pückler, who was leaning back with his buttocks against the desk. But he knew it was only making everything worse for himself. Pückler was white with anger, his lower lip quivering. He called Ralf an animal and stepped forward to kick him in the groin. Ralf doubled over in agony.

'You won't be needing your balls much here,' Pückler said.

Ralf became dizzy. He had to be carried downstairs, all the time feeling that he was going to be sick. He became aware that he was taken into the basement, or 'U-Boot'. With each step, his nostrils sensed the increasing dampness. A surge of hate ran through him as they pushed him forward through the corridor. 'You are worse than the Nazis,' he heard himself shouting. It echoed through the basement and lodged in the seeping walls. He didn't even feel the blows of the truncheons.

TWENTY-SIX

Claudia was worried about Mathias finding out. It was one thing concealing the meetings with Kevin, but going to a dinner party where Kevin and Mathias would sit around the same table with her would be a nightmare. Alexandra had arranged this dinner months in advance for Klaus's birthday and there was no way that Claudia could pull out now.

At the table, she seemed to be playing the role of Mathias's wife like an actor rehearsing for the stage. She avoided making direct eye contact with Kevin and watched for any signals, making the effort to listen more to Mathias when he had something to say. She was rather good at playing the role of his wife, she thought, hiding her love obsession so coolly. Occasionally, though, when she could no longer suppress her thoughts of the last sexual encounter with Kevin, sitting across his kness in the garden house and holding on to his head with both hands, she was glad that the discussion had taken on a serious note. To think about sex during the dinner, while everyone else was talking about the ecology, made her drunk with desire.

There were new faces around the table at Klaus and Alexandra's that night. An environmentalist had arrived with Dieter's sister Gabi. Otherwise, it was more or less the same intimate group. Out of courtesy, the newcomer had been allowed to bring up the Benetton ads all over again, and this was followed by a free-for-all invective with everyone denouncing low standards in the free market. Mathias laughed. He was the only dissenter. Claudia admired him for it, but she also feared the slight madness with which he took on the rest of the guests, deriding them, rebutting all their moral nonsense. She was afraid that he would suddenly round on her in the same way, as though he had personal reasons for being so hostile and difficult. The environmentalist looked shocked and continued to rail against all advertisers, making them out to be the new totalitarian force in the world. Mathias smiled.

'You must remember, there are no negatives in advertising, only redemption,' Mathias said calmly, and everyone suddenly looked at him as though he were some kind of new prophet. 'Advertising is full of hope – what religion used to have. What socialism once had.'

It turned into a heated talk-show debate, everybody trying to find a space to make their own emotional contribution, everybody personalizing the global catastrophe in a contest of predictions. Mathias remained the only adversary, snapping at everyone's convictions, and Claudia continued to get the feeling that he was doing so because he was really angry about her.

'I think we're all starting to feel the greenhouse effect here,' she intervened before she realized the unintentional irony of her own words.

She helped with the plates and found a chance to talk to Alexandra in the kitchen while she was brewing the coffee. Alexandra confided to Claudia that she and Klaus were finally intending to start a family.

'He's agreed,' she said, delight in her eyes.

Claudia didn't know whether it was too soon to congratulate her. 'That's great news, Ali,' she said.

'Nothing has happened yet. But we've been busy,' she said, winking at Claudia. 'We're keeping our fingers crossed.'

Mathias heard the news about Alexandra's future baby from Claudia when she came back to the table with the coffee cups. She whispered to him while nobody was looking and told him it was still a secret. Mathias was puzzled by the information, as though Claudia had offered him a few crumbs.

His suspicions had reached a new pitch since he had taken a trip out to the garden house. The previous evening he had driven out to Hohenschönhausen again and had gone into one of the Stasi apartment blocks on Grosse Legge Strasse near the prison. Acting on an old address he had received from a colleague, he went up to the fifth floor and found the name Pückler still written on the door. Pückler had lived within walking distance of the prison, though other people in the block confirmed that the apartment had been empty for at least two years.

Mathias realized that these were ex-Stasi people too, most likely people who had worked with Pückler or who knew him. He spoke to the caretaker and was told that the flat had been empty since the end of 1989. There was no forwarding address. They had sought new tenants for the apartment but people were reluctant to move to Hohenschönhausen.

On the way back in the car Mathias had made a diversion and driven to the lake. Instead of going back to the *Tageszeitung*, he went over to the garden house. He didn't know what to expect, whether he half imagined finding Claudia there with her lover. He felt his suspicions betrayed a kind of insanity. His detective work on Claudia struck him as uncivilized. Even the word adultery seemed so religious and outdated.

There was nobody at the garden house. Mathias unlocked the door and was greeted by the familiar musty smell of unaired interiors. There were dead bluebottles and other insects on the window sill. He checked the little stove, and the crockery. The beds seemed the same as ever, untouched. Nothing in the little house had changed. Outside, the plums lay on the ground around the tree, a further sign that nobody had been there.

He felt he had disgraced himself with his own paranoia. He left. And as he heard the squeak of the gate behind him, a neighbour came walking around from the other side along the path.

'Ah, it's you, Herr Hauser. You must have forgotten something.'

Mathias eyed his old neighbour in the bright blue shorts, white hair on his brown leathery chest, and suddenly both men seemed to clear up the misunderstanding for themselves. The neighbour must have said goodbye to Claudia earlier that day.

'Everything is in order,' the neighbour said, beginning to turn back on his heels. 'I was just wondering who it could possibly be . . . I was beginning to think somebody was breaking in.'

'You're very kind, Herr Kempinski,' Mathias said, smiling and holding up his briefcase. 'Just left this behind.'

TWENTY-SEVEN

At Hohenschönhausen, Ralf Krone's interrogation went on for weeks. Each spell of questioning ended with a period of time in the 'U-Boot' section where there was no daylight, no windows, no ventilation, and where he soon became completely disoriented. He had no idea what time of day it was any more. The food was worse than before. The beige walls were shiny with condensation because there was no heating.

He could never sleep. He was kept under constant light and told to stand. At other times it was constant darkness, pressing on his chest like an enormous weight. He was usually taken out for interrogation at night, when he was at his weakest, or when he had just begun to sleep out of sheer exhaustion. By the time he was returned to the cell, he could no longer remember what he had said to Pückler.

He craved water and his mind had begun to contort everything that had happened to him. He longed for the world outside and was exposed to the most random set of memories: science laboratories, trees, streets in Erfurt where he had walked as a boy. He dreamed about apples until apples began to flash in his head like a demented fruit harvest. He remembered the plots of books, and at times his consciousness reached a plateau of calm, only to be wrenched back abruptly by thoughts of Christa.

He refused to believe that she was upstairs in the same prison, as Pückler kept telling him. With maddening accuracy, he could still hear her calling out 'my husband, my husband' like a strange final echo. He had no defence against these intimacies of the past. Here in the darkness, breathing the air from which he had already drained any oxygen, air that was already colonized by the sweet, sickly stink of his own shit, he battled for control of his mind. He tried not to think of Christa in sexual terms, enforcing on himself a kind of strict prison morality which was vital for survival. He imagined there was no love in the world, even convincing himself that nobody out in the real world was fucking any more; that love had been completely eliminated from society.

He tried to behave rationally and pretended to play the piano, closing his eyes and concentrating on the keys, though he always got lost halfway through the *Moonlight Sonata*. He was occasionally flooded with guilt that he had not written to his parents more often.

The complete absence of sound filled him with a terror of himself and his own mind. The threats of repeated violence seemed like a great reprieve from this absolute exposure to himself. He suffered aural hallucinations, heard cars which were clearly not there. Goats. A river. One day he kept clearly hearing a dull wooden echo, something he imagined coming from a hollow pipe somewhere deep in a rainforest and which kept pushing him closer than ever to the precipice of suicide.

Then the lights would come on again, as though his only contact with humanity was this minimal communication through light. The slamming of doors and the arrival of food lifted his hopes, only to sink them again each time. His body was reaching deep into its stored reserves. The chronology of meals had been so utterly confused that he lost count of days and weeks, sure that Christmas had already come and gone without remark. He woke up once with the fantastic belated sound of bells in his ears, as though some neurological calendar rang out in his sleep.

Only his strict mental activities stood between him and madness now. He began to restrict these to brief sessions, so as not to exhaust the ability to concentrate. As well as the 'music room' he invented the 'maths room' and began to construct the

116

definitive science text book for schools, working at it for two hours or so every day. While walking on the spot in his cell in darkness he discovered the 'mind walk', in which he would imagine a walk around Erfurt, faithfully remembering the walls, houses, trees and street names.

But ultimately, any calmness achieved by this was destroyed instantly when he was brought before Pückler again. A sudden thaw in the interrogation seduced all his strength and willpower. Pückler would talk about freedom, reminding Ralf of all that he had thrown away in his life.

'You could have worked with us. You could have gone high up in the ranks.'

Pückler often generated a huge swell of self-pity in Ralf, speaking on and on about the treasures of the East German state. Inevitably, too, he would talk about Christa, how beautiful she was and how tragic the situation had become. Any mention of her name hit Ralf hard, reducing his silent defiance to nothing.

'She's beginning to show a bit now,' Pückler said once, making a round shape over his stomach with his hands.

Surely this confirmed that Christa was in Hohenschönhausen too. How else would Pückler know she had been pregnant? And with this small piece of explosive information Ralf was returned to the original cell. At last he was allowed to take a shower and to shave again. He found the heating on in his cell, and in this relative warmth he immediately got a cold which lasted for weeks.

When he recovered, he began to get active again, exercising and walking. For the first time in months, it seemed, he woke up at night and felt his involuntary nocturnal erection, an affirmation of health. But it only deepened his sadness, and was accompanied not so much by sexual desire as by a longing for the glossy memories of Western freedom. He had an image of the entire population of East Germany being in prison, jailors and inmates alike. From time to time he would silently curse the state. He was no dissident, but a reluctant idealist whose incarceration had made him an anonymous cold-war hero by default. Pückler confided that there had been some international outrage over Ralf's disappearance from West Germany. But he qualified this with great pleasure by telling Ralf that he would soon be liquidated anyhow. Pückler enjoyed making the guillotine sign.

'I'm surprised the order has not already come.'

Finally, Ralf's will broke down completely when Pückler produced the tape recording taken in Christa's old apartment back in Leipzig. In a new interrogation room, with nothing but a chair, a mirror and loudspeakers, Ralf was forced to listen to himself and Christa making love. Day after day the sound of their intimacies tortured him, accelerating his own delirium. He hated the arrogance of his own happiness in the past. It seemed like the ultimate indignity, this exposure to his own youth. And in this demented state, Ralf began to think of taking his own life. One morning, before daylight began to seep through the window above him in his own cell, he resolved to kill himself.

He thought of tearing up the sheets and hanging himself from the grid over the door, but the regularity with which the guards peered into his cell made this impossible. He had been hiding a metal spoon for days as a symbol of defiance. He tied his handkerchief around the spoon and sat on the floor with his back to the radiator. He placed the handkerchief around his neck and began to wind up the spoon at the back of his neck like a small propeller. When the handkerchief became so tight that he couldn't breathe, he lodged the spoon in the bars of the radiator, preventing it from spinning loose again. He felt the heat of the radiator on his back. Slowly he began to suffocate. His legs were kicking out and he blacked out just as the guards ran into the cell.

Two days later the cell door opened and Ralf saw Pückler standing there, triumphantly asking how the patient was. He surveyed the bruises around Ralf's neck. Ralf was weak and demoralized. He could hardly move. He smelled Pückler's aftershave and heard the squeak of his leather jacket. He felt Pückler's breath on the side of his face as he whispered in his ear.

'How dare you do this, Krone. Let me tell you, my friend, that privilege is reserved for us.'

TWENTY-EIGHT

Claudia offered to drive Mathias to the airport. He was going to Geneva on a *Tageszeitung* assignment. It was Saturday, and she had the time. In view of her own plans that weekend, this gesture of family solidarity felt a little hollow, and when Mathias turned it down and insisted on driving alone, she took his dismissal as a clear act of hostility. It was a further acknowledgment of crisis in their marriage, as though they couldn't bear to be in the same car together for so long.

Only a few days before that they had talked everything out, late into the night. It had all come to a head, and Claudia admitted that the problem between them was partly her fault because she had become so unhappy with her life; she found it difficult to express herself, but something had broken the spell of their relationship. Mathias spent hours attempting to isolate the cause of her discontent. Up to a point, he made it easy for her to speak honestly to him for the first time in months. But the only thing she refused to disclose was her affair with Kevin. They had not met in two weeks and she kept telling herself it was over. She no longer had anything to feel guilty about, so why mention it? But she knew that the fact that she concealed it meant that the affair would continue and that it still needed the protection of secrecy.

Mathias tried every angle. Was it him, was it the marriage, her job, the apartment, their friends? There had to be a source, and there had to be a cure. Inevitably, too, he discreetly touched on the possibility that she was meeting somebody, but she denied it.

In order to back this up, she began to point to dissatisfaction with her career. She wanted to do something new. She could not get over the feeling that she was trapped in her life: it was difficult to communicate her fears to Mathias, but there was something which made her feel numb and alone, even when they were together.

All in all, it had been not been an unsatisfactory discussion, even though they occasionally reverted to rounds of bitter counter-accusations. Each time, however, they managed, on that night at least, to bring it back to a healing session. Mathias made many suggestions: Claudia should get involved in something new, perhaps go back to university. He said they should go out together more often and it was time they both went away together alone, somewhere like Egypt, the USA, Ireland perhaps. They came towards each other. They talked about love and touched each other and made love, not out of any sense of obligation towards reconciliation but with a real feeling that they had temporarily conquered their differences. That night, they came as close to each other as ever was possible.

By Saturday, however, that attempt seemed to have come to nothing. His crude rebuttal of her offer to drive him to the airport allowed her to justify her planned meeting with Kevin. She shrugged her shoulders and walked away, feeling the unbearable distance between them again. In many ways she was glad that she would have the whole weekend with Kevin, and couldn't wait to see him and feel his arms around her. It was so uncomplicated and easy to be with Kevin. What made it even better was the certainty that it would end, that it was brief, that she would not have to stay with him for ever. Even though she felt increasingly guilty about her betrayal, the infinite claustrophobia of her marriage seemed to push her further into the affair.

Werner also appeared more indifferent towards her that morning. He was due to spend the weekend with Mathias's parents. Before he left with Mathias, however, Claudia wanted him to tidy his room. She found him playing his computer games, spoke to him, but got little reaction other than a muttered 'yes'. 'Did you hear me, Werner?' she said. Werner was lost in his game, as though surrounded by a thick, impenetrable mist. It felt like talking to a ghost. She became angry and strode over towards where her son was sitting. But along the way, before she placed her hands on his shoulders, she suddenly felt as if she had no right to be angry with him. It was she who had got lost in the fog.

Mathias had no intention of going to Geneva. His plan was to take Werner out to his parents' apartment in Alt Mariendorf and then spend a few days in Berlin on his own, working on the Christa Süsskind case and perhaps also finding out what Claudia was up to. He was obsessed by his discovery at the garden house and intended to catch her out rather than confront her with vague evidence.

He drove to Alt Mariendorf with Werner. He didn't like leaving his son there for too long because his own father was a bit of a racist, railing against 'Polaken' and 'Türken' defrauding Germany's social welfare system. Herr Hauser had carried the prejudice with him since the war, and whenever Werner came back from a weekend like this the politically correct, *Spiegel*-literate Claudia always demanded to know what racist garbage he had been fed by his ancestors.

Mathias had promised to buy his parents a new TV set on which to watch the athletics championships in Stuttgart. Germany was sure to clean up on medals. After dropping his mother and Werner at the supermarket, he drove around with his father. As usual on a Saturday morning the spirit of commerce reached a climax before all the shops closed for the weekend. But his father was being difficult about the TV. He would accept nothing but the best quality, insisting that no non-German TV would enter his home. 'None of these cheap Japanese products. I want something German,' he kept repeating, to the point of embarrassment.

Mathias's father went rigid when he was told that you couldn't find a good German TV set anywhere. They went through each single model in the shop. Nordmende was Dutch-owned, came the bombshell. The thin line of his father's lips demonstrated the depth of defeat as Mathias paid for the new Sony on his credit card. At home, while the new set was being unpacked and they heard the squeak of the white foam packing and smelled the newness from inside the cardboard box, his father sat in silence. Afterwards, Mathias negotiated between his parents over whether the cardboard box could not be put to good use, but his father wanted the damn Sony box out of the house as soon as possible.

By early afternoon Mathias was on his way to play tennis with a colleague. Werner was being taken to a new aqua centre with surf machines and loop-the-loop water slides. The lost look on Werner's face had given way to a minimal smile as Mathias held the boy's chin up to say goodbye. Mathias had never hit tennis balls so hard in his life as he did that afternoon.

By the evening he was back in Berlin, at Max Rodiger's apartment. He took a shower and then sat down for a while. He had brought some of his work with him, including the Christa Süsskind file. But he was suddenly confronted with a new emptiness, as though he would have to find something to do, as though he could not possibly fill in the time alone.

He wondered what would happen if he and Claudia broke up. Suddenly he could see a new vagrant life before him, with all its new burdens of belonging. He would be forced to find a partner, and though there were plenty of women he knew whose social lives were in free-fall, he went through a mental check list of possible dinner candidates and found nothing but a bleak forecast of impossible boredom. He even rehearsed various inane phrases like, 'How about Italian?' in his head, but each one struck him only as a highly obvious precursor to mindless, athletic sex with women he felt nothing for. He was afraid of a new life and clung to the idea that Claudia could be dragged back from the edge.

He left Max Rodiger's apartment at around 7 p.m. and drove out in the direction of the garden house.

TWENTY-NINE

After six months in detention at Hohenschönhausen, Christa became more heavy and slow with her pregnancy. The hysterical panic of the first months had given way to a dull boredom of the spirit. She became more detached and tranquil, floating on the intimate companionship with the baby inside her. The baby's movements placed her in a half-dream, like a constant anaesthetic.

She had cried all she could. She had no idea what had happened to Ralf. She knew only one thing, that she would wait for him through all of this, as though she possessed that primitive faculty of supreme patience which made it possible to continue through the loneliness and banality of time. Pregnancy made her immune to the taunts of the female wardens, to the degrading strip searches.

Every morning at 5 the door of her cell was flung open and she was led down the corridor towards the kitchen. Her walk was slow, almost regal. How often had she counted the neon lights and the diamond shapes of the lino, and the pattern of doors unlocking and relocking behind her all the way to where she reached the sudden reek of fat and stale soup in the kitchen? How often had she prepared the same *Eintopf*, every day, every week?

The long hours spent standing were excruciating on her spine. She still sometimes cried convulsively, not knowing how long she would be in prison. Once or twice she had thought of killing herself and the baby. But then, as the months passed, the baby became her only salvation.

She had more than once been informed by Pückler that there

was going to be a trial, but it never seemed to come. Nobody, not even the doctor, had said anything as yet about the baby's future, except some of the other female workers in the kitchen who told her the baby would be taken from her. 'You won't even see it,' they said.

She worried about Ralf. Pückler had said nothing about him except to make a sign with his index finger across his throat. Christa refused to believe it and sensed that he was alive in the same prison, perhaps only a few hundred metres away in another wing. Preparing the plates each morning she placed one extra piece of bread on one tray. Each midday she placed one extra lump of meat or an extra dumpling in one bowl, keeping Ralf alive in her thoughts, even though she understood the outrageous odds required for it to reach him.

She suffered heartburn. At night she dreamed of milk and apples. And escape. At times she began to see love as an escape. If her sortie to West Berlin with Ralf had been an attempt to elude destiny, then her imprisonment too, like her pregnancy, seemed to her a natural consequence of having loved too much. She regretted that she had not rejoiced more while freedom was so abundant. Life in prison reflected all the uncertainties of illness. It brought with it the same false hopes she had so often seen as a nurse in the eyes of patients, as though the whole prison institution were a disease: the walls, the grey steel doors, the threadbare blankets and the worn lino in the kitchen.

For a few days before the trial Christa was taken out into the sun for two hours a day. Though she didn't know it, it was to improve her colour, to make the accused appear as though she had been treated well. The trial itself was over almost before it even began. She was brought by van to the court. She had been offered her civilian clothes, though none of them fitted her, except the shoes. The court room was small, with red velvet curtains on the windows and a portrait of Lenin on one wall. The court was full of Stasi personnel. Behind a desk sat two men in plain clothes.

Ralf appeared through a door on the far side of the court. Their eyes met, not with any sense of affection or hope but with a mutual recognition of deep, intractable fear. It was a look that haunted her long afterwards. He seemed older, more gaunt, though his face too was brown from the sun. He was handcuffed and made to sit down behind a desk on the other side of the room, surrounded by guards carrying submachine-guns. She kept looking at him, hoping to receive some sign. But he was in a dream, not even listening when the charges were read out. Pückler handed a statement to the magistrate. Ralf was asked about the Zeiss money. He denied the charges and said nothing more.

Christa wanted to show Ralf some sign of her loyalty, and when she was asked by the magistrate about the money she stood up, allowing Ralf to see how pregnant she was, until she was pushed instantly back into her seat again.

The judge sentenced Ralf to fifteen years in Hohenschönhausen. Ralf seemed unmoved as he was led away towards the door. Then he stopped and looked back at her. 'Tell them about us, Christa . . .' he shouted. Then he was roughly pushed out through the door and, though she heard him shouting in the corridor, she couldn't make out what he was saying. She heard the magistrate sentence her to three years and recoiled at the shock. Her child would be almost going to school by then, she thought, bursting into tears.

Days later she gave birth. For once the guards were more understanding when she could no longer work in the kitchen. For once they didn't shout and the doctor was summoned to take a look at her. The midwife came and administered an injection. The handcuffs looked idiotic over the rounded arch of her stomach as she was taken from her cell, and all the time, as the baby was kicking, she wondered if all the fear in this environment would have an effect on it.

The familiar smells of the hospital came to Christa as a great sense of safety. She tried to speak to the nurses and find solidarity in their profession, but a warden standing by the bed ordered her to be silent. The midwife listened to her stomach as Christa looked at the woman's face, at the grey hair underneath the nursing cap and the gentle, reassuring hands around her tummy. She put all her trust in this silent authority.

Within hours she began to go into labour. Even then Christa wanted to keep the baby inside her, as though giving birth were like giving the baby away, like losing everything she had with Ralf. The midwife began to give instructions in a forceful voice, commanding her to push, and it didn't take long before Christa heard the baby crying out, a sweet lungful of air claiming a place for itself in the world.

Christa blacked out, and when she came round again the midwife was standing beside her.

'I'm sorry,' she said. 'We tried everything we could.'

'What do you mean?' Christa said.

'I'm so sorry, it was stillborn, my dear.'

Christa sat up. Even her physical exhaustion could not keep her down. 'It can't be true. That's a lie,' she said. 'I heard the baby cry just now . . .'

'Now come on, *Liebchen*. Don't upset yourself,' the midwife said, hovering around her with grotesque kindness.

THIRTY

As Mathias drove to the garden house on that Saturday evening, he openly admitted to himself that this was a low and degrading plot to lure Claudia out into the open with her lover. The Geneva assignment was a spurious set-up. In itself, it would be enough to kill his marriage for good, and he wondered if it was worth the risk in order to expose her.

He parked the car almost two kilometres away from the allotment and walked. He stopped along the way for a lousy *Schnitzel* at one of the overpriced restaurants near the lake, thinking every minute that Claudia and her partner would walk in and find him there, exposing him, rather than the other way around. The sun had gone down by the time he reached the garden house. There was no car parked by the gate and he took it that Claudia was either equally smart or she wasn't there. He opened the gate to the allotment in such a way that it would not squeak, reached the door of the house and found it locked. There was nobody around, and in many ways he found himself immensely relieved.

He began to weigh up the idea of going inside and waiting. It seemed too humiliating to think of himself lying in ambush in the dark, but then a crazy sense of excitement took hold of him, like a boy getting a kick out of hiding from adults, just for the sake of it. He unlocked the door and went inside without switching on the lights. The air inside the house assailed him once again with that fusty, uninhabited stillness. He locked the door behind him and slowly made his way up the stairs, until at one point the creaks in the wood shocked him into thinking that Claudia was already in the house. Only when he became accustomed to the absolute darkness caused by the closed shutters outside could he be certain that the house was empty.

He opened a can of beer and the ring almost exploded with a magnified crack under his finger, the noise of the liquid going down his throat amplified to the obscene. He sat down on Werner's bed. Then he walked around upstairs for a while, surveying the familiar geography under the skylights in the roof. It had all been designed while Werner was still a baby, when there was no need for doors, only a landing and a corridor between the two rooms leading to a tiny bathroom. Doors would have made the house too claustrophobic.

What he was now doing was absolutely psychopathic, Mathias told himself. His actions would drive Claudia away faster than anything she did herself. He hadn't thought the consequences through properly, and if anyone could see him standing in the dark, like a criminal in his own garden house, they would laugh their heads off. When he began to imagine the unbearable scene if Claudia did arrive, he made up his mind to leave immediately. He could be reasonable and talk to her instead. They could patch things up like adults. He decided to turn on the lights and walk out of the place, behaving like the real owner of the property he was. But just as he reached for the light switch he heard the squeak of the gate. He held back and listened.

There was a moment of self-induced terror. He hoped it was an illusion, perhaps the sound of a bicycle. But the squeak of the gate was unmistakable, and less than a minute later he heard the sound of voices as the door was being unlocked. He stood in shock at the top of the landing as Claudia walked into the living area below, speaking in English. How could she have anything to do with such a weedy specimen as Kevin? Even her choice of lover seemed to diminish Mathias's own status. Claudia laughed openly, unafraid and without any hint of shyness. Had Mathias expected her to be whispering?

He retreated cautiously into Werner's bedroom and hid behind the bed. The fact that he had put on no aftershave that evening seemed to make all of this very premeditated. He could no longer finish his beer, and the tension in his cramped position soon left him almost crippled. He waited in this trap of his own making for almost an hour, listening to the couple downstairs, wishing somehow that he could escape quietly and forget about it all. The Irishman below was remarking at the line of walking boots placed neatly by the door: father bear, mother bear and baby bear. Claudia laughed.

Mathias soon found himself listening to unexplained silences, followed by intervals of laughter and noisy kissing. Claudia was bringing Kevin up the stairs and they stalled halfway up for another intense exchange. Claudia's bracelets jangled, and when they finally reached the landing Mathias could see that she was already half undressed.

A small light went on in the bedroom, illuminating the landing in pink. It was the light by which Mathias had often made love to Claudia, making it all the more strange that he now lay half under the bed in Werner's room alternating between fury and sheer embarrassment, wondering if he should just get up and walk out before anything more serious took place. The moment filled him simultaneously with sadness as well as with an involuntary sexual desire which came with the light, an automatic longing produced by the sense of Claudia's lust. More than ever, he now regretted his own infidelities.

He should confront her now, he thought. But again he was immobilized by the sounds which began to emerge from the main bedroom. The little pink light went off again. Only the light from the moon came through the skylights now, and Mathias realized how Werner must have been exposed to their lovemaking in the past. The rooms desperately needed doors now. Mathias could not block out the sound, and the familiar shifting noise of the bed told him that Claudia and Kevin were already speeding along to the advanced rhythms of lovemaking. He could no longer endure the oppression of his confinement, as though he were in a coffin under the earth, or incarcerated in a cell. He left his hiding place quietly and began to move around Werner's small room, only to be drawn steadily towards the doorway by the vulgarity of Kevin repeating the word, 'Lovely, lovely . . .'

Suddenly Mathias began to think it was all very funny. He wanted to laugh out loud, walk out on the landing and tell Claudia how stupid she sounded when she was fucking in English. He would leave the house a hero. Claudia would come back to him like a lamb. But instead of going out brazenly and switching the lights on, Mathias edged his way to the door from where he could see Claudia and Kevin lying across the bed, the Irishman on top, his white Celtic buttocks working furiously in the light of the moon.

'I want you so bad, Kevin,' he heard her call out in her staccato German accent, and once more Mathias was ready to burst out laughing at her.

Watching the scene gave him a peculiar solidarity with the Irishman. It filled him with curiosity, as though this performance had bestowed him with the cheap erotic passion of a voyeur. This is what I look like, he thought. He could not watch these frenzied movements over Claudia's body with any great fury, only helplessness. He regarded Kevin not so much as a rival but as a version of himself, long ago. And the perverse idea came to his mind that he should take his own turn and make love to Claudia after the Irishman was finished. But he had already begun to regain a sense of disgust and wanted only to get out of the garden house as soon as possible.

He had come through a whole loop of emotions as a spectator of Claudia's passion. They had both cheated on each other and were now equal at least. As he watched the couple arrive at a climax, he felt detached, as though he were being shown how hurtful his own indiscretions had been to her; how stupid his own animal desires. He would never stand this test. If this was a trial of his love for Claudia, he had failed, because he felt nothing for her and wanted only the freedom of the streets outside.

He moved back into Werner's room and stood behind the wardrobe, an intruder in his own home. If he were discovered now, he no longer cared, because he had become indifferent to her. He would simply walk out.

The last cloying phrases of love were uttered in the other room, followed by an exotic, unbearable silence. He stood still for another thirty minutes until he was sure from the two distinct breathing patterns that Claudia and her lover were both asleep. Picking up the half-empty beer can, he began to inch his way down the stairs, avoiding all the known creaks as he had avoided any possibility of honesty between himself and Claudia. He became aware of the sweat under his arms and the dryness in his mouth confirmed a huge thirst. Opening the door of the house, he realized how suffocating the familiarity of this place was. He stepped outside and made it to the end of the path, pulled the gate silently behind him and walked away from his marriage like a thief.

THIRTY-ONE

Mathias descended into a trance of depression. He hardly slept at all that night, drifting aimlessly from one bar to another to get rid of the burning images of Claudia's betrayal, telling himself it was over with her and then, almost instantly, pleading with her to stop. He was confronted not so much by her breach of faith as by his own loneliness and inability to get close to anyone, as though a vast gulf had opened between him and all other people. The longer he went without talking to somebody, the more impossible it became to cross the divide. Apart from the minimal requests to bartenders he remained silent. When he woke up the following day he felt exactly the same. Sleep had done absolutely nothing. He had no interest in food. He had no interest in people, and his own misery had swollen to enormous dimensions.

That Sunday morning he found himself walking around the Tiergarten for the first time in years. Everywhere he saw people with dogs, children, footballs, frisbees, and couples lying on the grass. Turkish families had spread out their picnics and played their music on ghetto-blasters, little islands of hermetic festivity. A small group of skinheads walked along carrying beer cans, shouting. On some of the trees, warning notices had been placed, giving the rough sketch of a rapist: have you seen this man? Mathias walked until he saw the Brandenburg Gate and the tourists, before turning back. He had no idea what to do with himself. Retracing his route increased the panic of isolation even more.

He stopped for coffee in order to make a decision about

Claudia. He wanted to go home and shout at her, cry, plead with her, or just to punish her with silence. Then he wanted nothing to do with her, though the idea of striking out a new life of womanizing seemed even more depressing: he could find no appetite for the safari of endless parties, bars, art exhibitions, and couldn't bear paying all that attention to clothes, aftershave, fitness and fucking. He realized he would have to talk to Claudia, but not too soon. He would have to ride out the storm, perhaps leave her for a few days. At odd moments he was hurled into a huge feeling of pity for her, as though she was just as troubled as he was by all this. At other times he felt a surge of hatred and violence towards her lover, Kevin. But it diffused almost as quickly because Mathias knew Claudia's mind too well. The Irishman would not last, that was certain.

In a delirium of hurt, Mathias eventually resorted to work. On Sunday afternoon, after a meal which he could not even remember having, he went back to Max Rodiger's apartment. He had an address for Erwin Pückler in Hamburg which he had earlier dismissed as a non-lead: Pückler didn't live there; it was only a transient address. But suddenly Mathias felt it was a huge break and decided to drive all the way to Hamburg. Driving at least gave him an illusion of progression, though when he found the apartment block in Hamburg, Pückler's name was not even on the door, never had been. He made enquiries but discovered nothing, no description of Pückler, and as he drove back to Berlin late in the evening he felt real defeat.

In the following days, however, the instinct for work continued to conquer the need to confront Claudia. He phoned her once, pretending it was from Geneva, but the conversation was hollow. He told her he was exhausted with the work. She reminded him of Dieter and Stefan's party the following Friday and he said he would see her there. For three days he immersed himself exclusively in the monotonous torpor of documents and birth registers, and in the end, accidentally, he came across the first significant breakthrough in the Christa Süsskind case.

While going back laboriously over the records of former East Berlin maternity wards, eliminating the births in June, July and August of the year in question, he found the name Krombholz. He recalled how Christa had told him she had been induced by the midwife at Hohenschönhausen. It had given him a clue. If only to make sure that there was no record of Christa Süsskind, he sat looking through the names Bernhardt, Bodenholz, Meinhof, Feuchtwanger, Schmidt, until finally he came across an entry for Krombholz. Mother: Mareille Elisabeth. Date of Birth: August 8th. Sex: Male. Weight: 4.08 kilos. Father: Rainer Andreas. Father's Occupation: Electronic technician. Registrar on Duty: Anna Nothof.

Mathias became very excited about his discovery. Claudia's transgression seemed to fade out of existence. He wanted to drive to Christa's place of employment and tell her immediately, the buzz of journalistic achievement almost overshadowing the protocol of sensitivity. He considered telling her over the phone, but then thought it was better to meet her. One thing was certain: within minutes, the whole suffocating dilemma over Claudia had shifted out of focus.

'I think I have found out something about your baby,' he said cautiously. Christa wanted to know straight away, but Mathias persuaded her that it was better to talk over lunch. She couldn't meet for lunch so he suggested something after work, avoiding the term dinner, joking about the *Tageszeitung*'s generosity. Suddenly, he felt that his contact with humanity was restored.

They met at a small Italian place near Charlottenburg. As they read through the menu Mathias noticed her anxiety and brought up the whole subject straight away. He asked her about the Krombholzes, whether they spent much money on luxuries.

'They had no children?' Mathias asked.

'No,' she said. 'Mareille had a hysterectomy.'

'That's what I thought.'

Mathias pulled out a photocopy of the birth register from his inside pocket and handed it over to Christa. He could see that she was shocked by the information. Then she slowly placed the sheet of paper on the table and looked away, fighting back her tears. Mathias had to send the waiter back three times.

'I'm sorry,' he said.

'It's all right,' Christa said, composing herself. 'It's just that they were meant to be friends.'

They discussed this new information in the light of everything that had happened to her. When they finally ordered, the small practicality of food seemed to allow her to deal with the shock.

'You'll have to think quite seriously about whether you want to go through the courts,' Mathias said. 'If you want, I can get you a good lawyer.'

She agreed to think about it first. Over dinner, she became quiet and reflective, sometimes asking questions. She said she would no longer allow the past to destroy her present life. They got talking about other things, and in order to deflect from the gravity of the subject Mathias spoke about his son, Werner. He impulsively began to describe his own situation and how his marriage had failed. He didn't even feel any sense of alarm at the idea of speaking about his marriage in the past tense. He became cynical, hinting that marriage was an outmoded concept which was in decline everywhere. It was futile to assume permanence.

'I think there should be a renewable contract,' he said. 'Every three years. Maybe with a monetary incentive for endurance. After forty years you get a trip to Rio.'

Mathias paid for the meal. Christa insisted on buying him a drink in return; she wanted to thank him. Even if nothing came of the Krombholz discovery, at least it was good to have the information. In the long run, she said, she would feel better knowing the truth. They drove to Stadtmitte, to the Tacheles, and went into one of the shopfront bars which had sprung up in abandoned East Berlin properties. They chose 'Fruit and Vegetables', with its bleak, sludge-green GDR shop sign.

They stood outside, as the night was still warm. Across the street a large open parachute billowed from the windows of a squat. The relentless sound of a rave party emerged from one of the basements, along with a pulse of ultra-violet light. The bar was multi-denominational with students, theatre-goers, punks, heavy metal fans and neo-hippies. There were prostitutes walking up and down along the street. Every now and again a car pulled up and one of them would disappear. Life was transient, everything coexisting perfectly in this new evolution of needs.

'Wild place,' Christa remarked.

'Yes. Something about the atmosphere I like,' Mathias said.

Christa got slightly drunk. She occasionally referred to Rainer and Mareille Krombholz, saying how hard it was to accept that friends could do such a thing. When it got cooler he suggested another bar further along the street. With more alcohol, he feared that he might take advantage of the crisis in his own life by pursuing his attraction to Christa, particularly in those moments when she became introverted and would shake her head in sheer confusion at the news about Rainer and Mareille Krombholz. It was as though she had to keep drinking to understand.

The new bar was like an exhibition of GDR artefacts: bits of old shop signs, a defunct Soviet washing machine, colanders, a headless tailor's dummy and the disembodied parts of a Trabi, all deconstructing the recent past like a post-modernist gallery. Later, when it began to approach closing time, Mathias knew he would not be able to drive and offered to get her a taxi instead. '*Tageszeitung*,' he laughed.

They were finishing their beer when a man came up to them and pointed at his wrist. Above the noise, Mathias heard him say, 'Time please.'

'Yes, OK . . . we're just finishing our beer here,' Mathias said, holding up his bottle.

It was hard to communicate with the music. There were other people still drinking, but the man didn't go away. 'Time please,' he repeated, again pointing at his wrist. Mathias stared at him furiously until Christa intervened, looking at her watch.

'It's almost one o'clock,' she said to the man, and he finally went away. Then she started laughing hysterically, throwing her head back.

'I thought he was . . .' Mathias began.

'Don't worry,' she said, putting her hand on his shoulder. 'I think he's far more embarrassed than you are.'

THIRTY-TWO

Claudia continued to feel a dangerous mixture of recklessness and guilt. At times she considered confessing everything. After the long and passionate weekend with Kevin, something urged her back to the safety of her own life. She thought long and hard about everything, realizing more than ever how much she needed a constant companion. She confided everything to Alexandra. 'I feel just like shit,' she said numerous times, trying to explain the depth of deceit. She wanted to put everything straight with Mathias: she loved him, there was no question of it, even though she still needed to keep the escape route to Kevin open a while longer.

How could she tell Mathias? How could she hurt him? Laying these sordid facts out before him would be worse than the initial betrayal. On top of everything, the injury to his pride and his whole sense of broken trust would be worse than any misdemeanour she had already entered into. In the end, Claudia resolved to end the affair and tell Mathias nothing. It was much easier to tell Kevin it was over; he would understand her decision.

During the week, she took her mother out shopping. She took Werner to the swimming pool and, afterwards, out to his favourite diner. She found time to read and to write a few letters, all of which began to give her the assurance that everything would soon return to normal. In a way, she already felt sad about the end of the affair, a feeling which seemed to coincide with the summer's coming to an end.

She decided to change her hair; nothing severe, just a light cut and a bit of colour. For Stefan and Dieter's party, she told herself. But when she came home from the hairdresser she thought they had put in far too much red and became defensive about it. She had to meet Alexandra again the night before the party, just to put her mind at rest. It was not Kevin she was so anxious about but Mathias.

'I don't know what came over me,' she said when she saw Mathias at the party. He had come straight from the airport. They embraced and kissed, as though nothing was wrong.

'Do you like it?'

As if her hair mattered more than her body, and her love, she thought. Mathias seemed to stare at her in shock. The colour was either flaming red or bright copper, he thought, proving that the extent of her Irish involvement had literally got into her hair.

'Come on, Matt. It can't be that bad,' she said when he hesitated.

'No. It's stunning,' he said immediately. But the word dropped like a smashed wine glass between them.

The party was being held in Stefan's car workshop, in honour of an AIDS patient. The garage atmosphere had been accentuated, though the smell of oil and diesel was masked by the contradictory atmosphere of cigarette smoke and food, as well as a cloud of aftershave, hair-oil and male body lotion. Balloons and large cards with best wishes hung all around the walls along with tyres, fan belts and other accessories. A motorbike belonging to the AIDS patient had been suspended on chains from the ceiling, lit by green and pink spotlights and pivoting around occasionally when somebody jumped to touch it. In the background there were engines and wheels and motor parts everywhere. Dieter and Stefan both ran around in boiler suits with the seats cut out of them. Along with a mixed crowd of men and women, there were many other gay men at the party, including the shockingly guant figure of Botho Bischof in his wheelchair, for whom the party was being held. Stefan at one point silenced the gathering to make an emotional speech, bringing many people to the verge of tears when he referred to the occasion as a farewell party. Dieter recorded everything on video.

For obvious reasons, Kevin and Claudia stayed apart throughout the evening, standing at opposite ends of the garage, eating their food separately. Mathias ate with Claudia and, for some reason she found the intimacy of sharing food with her husband unbearably strained. They talked about their son: Claudia said Werner wanted Mathias to take him to a football match, but then their conversation became merged with that of the other guests at the party.

Mathias could see how Claudia was avoiding Kevin. She practically ignored the man altogether and her discomfort strangely contributed to his own extraordinary liberty at the party. It had begun to act on him like a powerful narcotic, raising him up high above the clandestine fog of deceit which enveloped Claudia and her lover. He was as free as a bird himself, sparkling with honesty and virtue.

Kevin stood beside the bar, which had been constructed on the back of an old Second World War vintage truck without wheels. When Claudia became engaged in conversation, Mathias decided to go and talk to him as though nothing was wrong. The strain of Kevin's awkwardness bordered on hostility. There was little eye contact between them, even as they spoke with gravity about the imminent death of the AIDS victim. Mathias felt no animosity; in an odd way, he realized that he had always liked Kevin; they could have become good friends, or at least occasional drinking pals, he thought. Mathias unveiled his plan to abandon all caution and get drunk.

'I'm just going to get fucking arseholes,' he said in English, asking Kevin if he had pronounced the phrase properly.

Kevin repeated the term, demonstrating that the emphasis was not so much on the 'fucking' as on the 'arseholes'. The two men drank furiously together to erase the discomfort, entering into a sweeping series of clichés; talking football, rock music, the nature of crowds, all of which seemed to bring Kevin out of himself and turn them both into boozing companions. Mathias wanted to know all the different Irish terms: plastered, paralytic, bollocksed, skulled, scuttered . . .

'Skuttered, skuttered, skuttered,' Mathias repeated a number of times, but he could never get the intonation quite right, no matter how fast he drank.

Claudia was concerned at the apparent camaraderie between them. She could see them talking, but was afraid to go over herself in case Mathias suspected something. She felt that Kevin was already gone from her life and thought that she would remember him as a nice man: generous, quiet; a good listener and a good singer. She would remember the spiritual, or rather poetic, environment around him, even when he was funny. She sent Alexandra over to find out what they were talking about, but Mathias was behaving like the most reasonable jilted lover of all time. And the fact that Alexandra had come over like that only gave Mathias the idea that she was an accomplice to Claudia's affair, just keeping her mouth zipped like an informal operative.

All the time, guests were shaking hands with the man in the wheelchair and coming away moved to tears. The oily floor had been covered with a tarpaulin and people were starting to dance. In a quieter part of the workshop, Claudia went to kiss him and speak to him, coming away moments later in a flood of tears, knowing that the grief of the occasion had become confused with her own emotions. When she heard this man speaking to her in his tiny, weak voice, she could not hold back.

'Botho told me to dance. He told us all to dance,' she said, as though she were conveying the words of a saint. She repeated the same message to everyone at the party, even to Mathias, each time coming up with a new wave of tears to conceal her own real tears.

To demonstrate the message, Claudia began to dance with great energy. She was joined by Mathias, who was already more drunk than she had ever seen him before. He danced in a most provocative way, his chaotic choreography causing laughter among the other dancers. Alexandra and Klaus showed concern. Claudia kept dancing with her eyes closed. Every now and again the music turned to gay themes, and the gays at the party all put on a show of solidarity. At intervals, Mathias went back to the bar to get more drink, speaking to Kevin, who had become glued to the spot.

'Come out and dance,' Mathias commanded, and the Irishman had no option but to follow him on to the dance floor. Claudia was horrified when she opened her eyes and found the two men dancing together before her. 'Lovely,' Mathias kept remarking in English, but neither of them picked up the message.

Mathias was being obscene again, thrusting his hips forward in a comical rhythm that defied the musical beat. And the suit he was wearing made the whole thing even more absurd. With his status as the wronged husband and his untouchable virtue, he had become completely uninhibited, embracing Claudia, whispering, and then licking her ear before she pushed him away and left the dance floor.

'Mathias, I'm leaving if you carry on like this.'

She went up to the bar and got herself a drink, furious. She held the bottle in her hand and watched as Mathias turned to dance with Kevin again. She began to realize that Mathias must know something. Moments later, the two men left the dance floor and came towards the bar, ignoring her as though she didn't exist. Only Kevin gave her an anxious, loving glance as they opened new bottles. But it seemed as though beer was far more important than love, or jealousy, or any other plane of human interaction. As though in getting drunk together, men achieved a form of communication superior to sex and music and literature and all other avenues of expression.

The music over the giant speakers sent tremors through the floor of the workshop. Now the remaining dancers on the floor collectively decided to form a train together, each person holding on to the next person's waist, all blindly following the leader.

The train gathered more and more static onlookers as it progressed like a giant caterpillar to the music. Claudia refused to join in. To Mathias, this kind of dance train had always represented the worst fascist idiocy he could imagine. He had avoided them at conferences, at night clubs, at press parties and on holidays; he could never submit to the utter mindlessness of this Euro-fun. But next time the chain train came along they would all be sucked into it; even if only for the sake of the dying AIDS patient, they would be unable to refuse.

Mathias thought fast about avoiding it. He toasted Claudia and winked at her. She looked away, still angry, knowing that a confrontation was due. Mathias watched the train getting bigger and bigger, weaving its way around all the artefacts of the garage, picking up more and more reluctant dancers in its demonic progress, every one of the participants smiling as though they were part of some kind of great institutional childishness, acting on newly imposed Euro-laws of happiness. Somebody thought of the brilliant idea of putting Botho Bischof in his wheelchair right up at the front of the train, and now there was no excuse to stay away. Klaus and Alexandra were already shouting to them all to join in.

'Grab hold there,' they demanded, like voices from a party-line commercial. 'Come on, you people.'

And as the train came around slowly, with the dancers throwing out their legs alternately on each side, Mathias felt its terrifying power approaching and prepared for flight. He turned to see if he could get away. He had visions of Claudia and himself and Kevin all holding on to each other in a nauseating procession of blind acceptance. As the train turned the last bend on its way back towards the bar, his head seemed to jolt back in a sudden crisis. He was scuttered, he said to himself, but he would still have to escape this madness, and with a devious burst of malice he turned to Kevin, still standing beside him.

'Save me from this fucking train,' he said in English, once again wrongly placing the emphasis on the 'fucking'.

'I'm not making an eejit of myself either, no fear,' Kevin responded.

Mathias placed his arm around the Irishman. He felt him going rigid with discomfort. Claudia saw it happen but could do nothing in time to stop it.

'We'll stick together,' Mathias said to Kevin, and before the Irishman could answer, Mathias put his face up to him and kissed him. Kevin's mouth was open in shock, and Mathias went all the way, thrusting his tongue right down into his mouth. It was like singing without sound. Mathias had no idea where this absurd urge came from, only that it was entirely spontaneous and that his tongue was now suddenly rammed deep into Kevin's throat, preventing him from speaking or even gasping with surprise.

At that same moment, before Claudia could intervene, the train passed by, sucking her up somewhere in the middle between Alexandra and Klaus, from where she could only look back in horror at the sight of Mathias kissing her lover. Kevin spat Mathias's tongue out again with the most intense disgust, like a piece of foul-tasting meat. The Irishman staggered back and knocked over some bottles at the bar. The look on his face was one of fury and utter incomprehension.

'I wouldn't hit you,' he said, raising his fist. 'For her sake.'

Mathias already wore a wide, benign smile, more like the expression of a clown, calmly diffusing any possibility of violence.

'Fuck off, you bastard,' Kevin said predictably. It all sounded so hollow. He stood there trying to think of something more agressive, more hurtful, something that would proclaim his own manhood.

'She's a great fucking ride,' he muttered, just before he walked unsteadily away from the party, carrying Mathias's grin with him as he went.

Claudia freed herself from the train and stood for a moment looking over at Mathias, then followed after Kevin.

THIRTY-THREE

The real confrontation between Claudia and Mathias began over the phone the next day when she finally managed to track him down at work for a short, vicious exchange. It was difficult for either of them to be reasonable. All the dirt was thrown out and it soon degenerated into a series of raging accusations followed by deep interludes of hostile silence which meant far more than anything they could say.

'What bothers me, Claudia, is how you kept lying to me. How can I ever believe you again?'

She sighed, and echoed these clichés with others of her own, more like the lines of a soap opera to which they had been condemned and from which they would never be able to extract themselves. The words made everything ordinary. And phrases which they would normally have laughed at together now took on new meaning. He wanted to know how long it had been going on. She wanted to know how he had found out and mentioned his past infidelity. He asked her how far she was going to go. Now and then she came close to crying, but wouldn't allow herself to submit. She wanted to know where he had stayed that night, but when, more to the point, he asked her the same question, she refused to answer as it would give him the edge. She asked him if he had moved out. 'Mathias, we'll have to face each other,' she said. But Mathias didn't want to meet her because he didn't want to be reasonable. It was all too important a matter to be talked out so soon, as though he refused a face-to-face confrontation for fear that he might see her side of things.

It would require an enormous, almost superhuman effort for them ever to get back together again, Claudia thought. Neither of them had the strength or the stamina to initiate a reunion, let alone talk of forgiveness or love. There was strength enough for hate, and tears and suffering and jealousy, nothing but weakness when it came to crossing that gulf between them.

And that was only the first phone call. All in all, Claudia phoned him three times that Saturday, and it was not until the last of these, as they talked about Werner, that either of them became rational. When it came to home management, they both still showed extreme dedication. Werner was staying with Mathias's parents again, and Mathias agreed to collect him there on Monday afternoon.

There were further phone calls the following day, when Claudia found the number of Max Rodiger's apartment. But even when she finally hinted that it was all over with Kevin, it did nothing to bring them any closer together. Mathias laughed, cynically; hurtfully. It was Claudia who produced the superhuman strength needed for reconciliation, even driving over to Max Rodiger's apartment on Sunday evening. But Mathias was out and she bitterly regretted any idea that she had capitulated, because he seemed to be desperately holding on to his advantage.

She went back to Kevin.

On Monday afternoon, Mathias drove out to collect Werner. He too was aware of holding on to his hurt status for a purpose. He had made up his mind to phone Christa, but how, and under what pretext, he didn't know yet. Perhaps he should let her meet Werner briefly. It struck him that it would be nice for Christa to see the fatherly side of his nature; he was blatantly using his son as bait.

He phoned her from Alt Mariendorf, with his own mother listening through the half-inch gap in the kitchen door. It was here as an adolescent that he had made his first cautious phone calls to girlfriends. His father was in the sitting room with

Werner watching the world athletics: 3,000-metre heats, interrupted by discus throwing.

Christa agreed to meet Mathias after work. He became light-headed. He had not felt this kind of excitement in years. His mother then forced him to sit down to a massive slice of cake before Mathias eventually got ready to leave again and extracted Werner from the living room. His father raised his backside two inches off the sofa to say goodbye. Mathias noticed that the English commands on the remote control had already been superimposed with German tags.

'Can I stay with you, Papa?' Werner asked on the way home. He was holding the take-away pizza in a cardboard box on his lap and the smell was filling the car. It was an awkward moment. Claudia must already have spoken to him about all the trouble on the phone.

'We can't do that to your mother, Werner,' he said. 'She's expecting you.'

But it demonstrated how well Werner understood the adult world of break-ups, and how he had almost anticipated it, far in advance. Many of his friends at school had been through it before and it seemed only that Werner had arrived late. When they collected Christa on the way she talked mostly to Werner. It seemed easier to talk to a boy. And it concealed any awkward signals. She was a good listener and wanted to learn everything about computer games. 'Enjoy your pizza,' she said to him when they arrived at the apartment block. Mathias was careful not to meet Claudia. He took Werner as far as the front door and called the lift.

Over dinner, Mathias told Christa stories about his son, how he was afraid of jelly as a child and would actually run away from the wobbly mass. It seemed as though this boy had won her heart over. The only thing that bothered Mathias was the thought of Max Rodiger's apartment, the narrow strip of mirror on the ceiling of the bedroom, and the mirrored tiles in the bathroom. He wanted everything to appear less deliberate.

148

Only the offence to Claudia, that was deliberate.

'Why don't we have coffee at my place?' he offered. It was perfectly natural.

'Why not?' she said, without even thinking.

The lights were beginning to come on in all the apartments when they arrived. Christa whistled at the size of the living room as she sank down into one of the leather sofas. Mathias admitted that it wasn't his apartment and made it sound as though he had broken up with Claudia years ago. 'We're still good friends,' he lied.

He spilled half the coffee beans on the floor as he spoke from the kitchen. Then with a great explosion of noise the CD player came on in the living room, and he ran in to show her how to switch it down as Christa stood there with her hand over her mouth. It felt as though the whole story with Ralf was starting all over again, more peacefully, in a new Germany, even though they were now committed to ignoring each other's personal history. He wondered why he had not made this move long ago. Perhaps he had always seen her as an older woman.

He wanted to play music for her, beginning with something she knew and moving on to tracks he had become obsessed with over the past few days. He moved about like a distracted DJ, thrilled to find somebody who appreciated him. And every time he found a track she recognized it was like an electric meeting of minds, as though it allowed them to look into each other's eyes. Christa got up and went to the window to look down into the street. He followed, and began to dance with her, in full view of the people in the apartments on the other side. It didn't matter. They had witnessed more dramatic things.

He was no dancer, Christa felt. But he wasn't clumsy either, just a little boisterous, pulling and turning her around the floor in a series of firm, erratic movements which made her laugh out of sheer helplessness. Had the drink affected him so much? He was gentle one moment and incredibly forceful the next. She thought it was some kind of joke at first, though he wasn't smiling. As he released the clasp and allowed her hair to fall down around her shoulders, he seemed to have taken control of her, tacitly commanding her to surrender all authority to him. He said very little except to call himself 'Nureyev'. She was out of breath, and he watched her shoulders moving up and down for a while before he took her in his arms and kissed her, first her forehead, then her mouth. It was all a bit paternal, she felt, but when she began to give herself to the kiss he broke off abruptly and went back to swinging her around in expanding circles towards the door, pulling her into the bedroom where she stood for a moment, utterly speechless. She didn't notice the strip of mirror on the ceiling till much later. All she saw were the photographs of Hohenschönhausen; dozens of black and white prints of herself in that cold, grey detention centre stuck to the walls around the bedroom. She tried to work out the fixation, but remained silent. She just stood motionless, looking around at this gallery of prison shots as though she had been singled out as some kind of victim. He had switched off the light so that only the blueish glow from the corridor seeped into the room now.

Mathias noticed that she had become uneasy. 'Investigative journalism,' he said, dismissing the exhibition with a little laugh. Then he took her hands and explained that he had been thinking about her for such a long time, ever since she had walked into his office. He showered her with reassuring words and kisses around her face and neck. He sat her down, then pushed her back on the bed, staring into her eyes, his hand holding her face in a vice grip. She put up no resistance and he began to remove her clothes with a kind of reckless urgency that made it look like he'd studied the photographs with that intention. He trapped her underneath himself, pinning down her arms, realizing for the first time why he had become so obsessed with her; she had the qualities of a captive. He could love her in a way that he could never love Claudia.

THIRTY-FOUR

In Hohenschönhausen after the trial, Christa Süsskind and Ralf Krone continued to be interrogated. The only difference was that, since they had been sentenced, the questioning now took on a more salacious nature. Erwin Pückler knew private, intimate details about Ralf and Christa which he could not have gleaned from any old tape recordings or transcripts.

In Ralf's besieged state, knowing that not even the first year of his sentence had been completed, he took these things very badly. From some of the details which either he or Christa must have given away under pressure, Pückler had put together a formidable dossier on their relationship. How could Pückler possibly know that Ralf and Christa made love on the train once coming back from the coast? Or that Christa had her first pubescent orgasm rocking back and forth on her aunt's piano stool? How could Pückler know that Ralf always had an urge to walk after lovemaking, either up and down the bedroom in the dark while Christa was already asleep, or sometimes actually getting dressed and walking out in the street?

Ralf tried to come to terms with his isolation. He refused to fall into the clutches of religion and took whatever solace he could from his mental exercises, his meals, his daily routine – the sound of doors, of dogs barking, the glorious act of pissing, the feeling of water on his hands and face, all became precious rafts of reality. Each trip down the corridor was like a voyage out into the world, and at times it seemed he could manage fifteen years if only Pückler had not begun on this new line of questioning.

'Did you see your relationship with Christa Süsskind as subversive or supportive of our state?' was the kind of thing Pückler wanted to know, claiming that it was part of an important state investigation.

Ralf refused to answer most of these enquiries. Pückler explained that if he co-operated, he could make things easier on Christa and himself; the state might be persuaded to make concessions, such as finding him some work.

'She had multiple orgasms, didn't she?' Pückler remarked slyly.

Ralf stared at him.

'She said so herself. It's written down here,' Pückler insisted.

Ralf was reminded that Christa was being interrogated too. At first, he took this statement as a sign of her wonderful defiance, but then it, too, began to oppress him. He cursed the state and Pückler warned him not to risk spending his entire time in the 'U-Boot'. Then he paused and leaned across the table towards Ralf. 'So, did she ever tell you that she had a multiple orgasm?'

Pückler persisted. He wanted to know about their proclivities, bedroom props, if sex was better while they were on the run in the West. Did their sexual relationship change after her pregnancy? He asked about the frequency, about infidelity, about marriage.

Every small act of rebellion was punished with a spell in the 'U-Boot'. And each bit of co-operation was rewarded. Sometimes Pückler interpreted Ralf's silence as an admission to his question, and the dossier became more and more a product of Pückler's imaginative interpretation. Initially the rewards came in small measures, like an extra shower, an extra blanket, clean underwear. Later he was given work transcribing documents for the prison doctor.

A small desk was placed at the end of Ralf's cell. At first the desk was taken away at the end of the day and the sheets of paper were all counted. But then, incredibly, things became more relaxed. The desk stayed and the paper was no longer counted, allowing Ralf occasionally to hide one or two of the sheets in his cell. He wrote anti-state slogans. Then he began a letter to Christa. When he realized that nobody really missed the paper at all, he began to write his autobiography, an act which gave him a feeling of strength he had not had in a long time.

The autobiography remained undiscovered. The papers piled up underneath the bunk bed. A month went by and nobody had tampered with them. This ability to create made up for most other deprivations; it would keep him alive, and one afternoon he sat at his desk in tears at the sheer satisfaction of finding words to describe the injustices.

Meanwhile, Ralf was also sustained by his contacts with the prison doctor, though their conversation was limited to the doctor's terse instructions. The interrogation sessions also became less frequent. But then, one afternoon, Ralf was taken from Pückler's office and led through corridors into another wing, where he was placed in a new cell. He was devastated. The idea of losing his autobiography was worse than anything he could imagine. Nothing in the new cell gave him solace and he realized that he had invested too much in his work.

The evening dragged on. As he drew back the blankets he found a familiar object: one of Christa's long, oversized T-shirts. He was in her cell, he discovered. Lying down, he became overwhelmed by doomed excitement. He could think only about her and pressed the T-shirt against his face, inhaling her scent like some sweet, faint caramel. His erection felt like something outrageous; grotesque. He put the T-shirt away and forced himself to think of the skin diseases he was transcribing for the doctor.

The guards on the morning shift seemed surprised to find him there. 'How did you get in here?' a female warden shouted behind him. He rarely saw any of their faces.

Back in his own cell he set about the medical work again. Later he turned to his autobiography and discovered that the papers had been tampered with. Had they been read by the guards? He found a long blonde hair on the blanket. And a second one. There could be no doubt, they had been deliberately switched.

Pückler laughed about the incident. 'Imagine, you two being put in the wrong cells,' he said. 'Bring back pleasant memories then?'

Ralf tried to put the incident out of his mind. Only Christa's hair, hidden among the pages of his autobiography, remained as proof that it had happened. He might even have submitted to the accident theory if not for the fact that, some days later, he saw Christa in real life at the other end of the corridor. They saw one another for a split second before she was rushed away through the end gates. He had never seen any other prisoner. And her above all people. The red light went on at the end of the corridor and he was promptly pushed back to his cell. As he sat there, in a new chronic state of near madness, no longer able to piece together any of his thoughts, he began to fear that his whole relationship with Christa might have been a mere illusion.

THIRTY-FIVE

In February, on Stasi Day, it was the custom for prisoners to receive a piece of cake and a mug of real, ground coffee, the scent of which filled each cell and reaffirmed the unlimited scope of lost pleasure. For some it came each time as a delicious concession, reminding them of home and the simple happiness of freedom. For others it came as a grotesque spirit of commemoration which only underlined the misfortune of their imprisonment. In general, the food in Hohenschönhausen was designed just to keep the inmates alive. They were weighed once a week to ensure that the food, in combination with lack of exercise, didn't increase their weight. Whenever a slice of cake was brought around to the cells, some of the prisoners consumed it within minutes. Some took at least an hour, allowing the slow, dreamy process of digestion to hang like a magical plumb weight in the stomach. Others, like Ralf, refused to touch this cynical gift from the state and hurled it with sheer fury at the light above the cell door.

It fell to Christa and other female prisoners to apportion these gaudy cakes in the kitchen. As always, she cut one larger slice in the hope that it went to Ralf, but this act of random favouritism had begun to frighten her, as though it would awaken an absurd desire in the wrong person. What if Ralf were no longer there?

On the evening of Stasi Day she was taken to the washrooms and told to take a shower. The wardens had replaced her prison smock with the civilian clothes she had been wearing at the time of the abduction. Even the sight of these sent a potent rush of excitement to her head and she asked if this meant she was going home, but was brusquely reminded not to speak.

She was taken to a room which had been furnished with two armchairs and a bed; unbelievable luxury, she thought. She didn't trust herself to sit down. When the door was locked behind her she stood staring at the clock above it, then cautiously approached a big mirror feeling her face and hair with a bewildered look. Her clothes were loose, and ill-fitting. Her cheeks had hollowed out.

Behind the one-way mirror in the next room sat Pückler, making notes. From Christa's behaviour, he deduced that she was not suspicious but introverted. He wrote down each reaction in detail. Then he put down the exact time, 9.14 p.m., and the exact conditions of the room. The light over the door had been left on.

Christa turned her back on the mirror as though she could no longer bear to look at herself. The room was cold and she felt the luke-warm radiator with her hand. Then she half sat down on the wing of a chair and waited with her arms folded, ready to jump up again at the least sound coming from the door.

Pückler then gave the signal for Ralf to be brought up. Ralf was preoccupied by the sudden fear that his own cell was being searched and that his book would be confiscated. He looked tired. Even when he was pushed into the cell with Christa he seemed lost and could only stare at her, unable to appreciate her presence in the same room.

'They took the baby,' was all that Christa could say to him, in a flat voice.

'Was it a boy or girl?' Ralf asked.

'I don't know . . .'

They remained silent as Ralf slowly began to examine the contents of the room. He stared at the clock as if he no longer understood the concept of time.

'Are you going home?' he asked, noticing her clothes.

'I don't know,' she said. 'I haven't been told anything.'

'Why else would you have your clothes back?' he said. 'Maybe they're letting us say goodbye?'

'There's eighteen months left . . .'

Christa retreated against the radiator. Ralf looked into the mirror. Each piece of dialogue between them so far marked only what separated them, not what had once been a shared life. The baby seemed like a fantasy; the entire history of their former intimacies irrelevant, if not completely forgotten. If anything, those past intimacies conspired to prevent them from communicating or accepting each other as real. They were like any two prisoners placed together: Ralf in his prison fatigues, Christa marginally closer to the outside world in her civilian clothes, facing each other with the impenetrable barrier of captivity between them. Each of them was locked into their own individual sense of hope or misfortune. They had never been further away from each other.

In the next room, Pückler continued to make notes. He observed that the couple had not made any gesture of affection towards one another. They were wasting precious moments together, showing little desire for interaction; no pity, no sadness, or any other emotion. They seemed preoccupied and self-absorbed, Pückler wrote. Once more, he noted the time: 9.56 p.m.

'Did you get the cake?' Christa asked.

'Yes, but I never eat it,' Ralf replied.

'I work in the kitchen, you know.'

'I didn't know that,' Ralf said.

He told her that he had been given work with the prison doctor. He began to pace up and down as though he could not wait to get back to it. They spoke haltingly about life inside the prison, like two people turned prematurely old, only partially aware of each other's existence. Memory was like a virus which had to be fought off. Talk of anything outside the prison would have come as a great, unbearable assault on the layers of self-protection they had developed for themselves.

157

'Do you hear the dogs?' Ralf asked her.

'No,' she said.

There were no dogs. But Ralf stopped pacing and waited to see if she could hear anything. Propelled more by fear than by anything else, he suddenly walked over to her and took her hand in both of his. He stared into her eyes. It was almost a hostile moment. He wished to say goodbye silently, without a word, just in case they never saw each other again. Pückler noted this development with great interest. It was a moment which, outside the prison, might have brought Ralf and Christa closer together than they had ever been before. But here, Christa's eyes only stared back with blank emptiness. It was impossible to give or accept comfort. Ralf let go of her hand and walked to the other side of the room. He stood by the door as though waiting to be let out.

Pückler wondered if these latest developments would inevitably lead the subjects back to love. He ordered the main light to be switched off. A table lamp cast an orange glow around the room and, but for the austere beige walls and the thick, opaque glass window, the room might have looked like any apartment bedroom. The heating was turned up and the pipes began to click and jump with expansion. Christa moved away from the radiator and sat down on the bed in the corner.

Pückler wrote a paragraph on room temperature, postulating the search for warmth and comfort as a key element in love. Everything had been done to create the illusion of freedom – lighting, homely furnishings, Christa's clothing. The test would soon show results. The heat had begun to embrace the prisoners in a drowsy cosiness, dragging down all resistance. Music played softly over two speakers high on the wall above the mirror. Neither of them had been seduced by such sounds since the arrest. Christa sat back. Ralf resumed walking up and down. Eventually, he sat down on the edge of one of the armchairs and talked to her quietly. He asked her what she would do when she got out. Would she go back to Halle or Leipzig? The conversation was like part of a distant dream. She told him she would look for the baby.

'What kind of a man is this?' Pückler remarked eventually, after a quarter of an hour had gone by with nothing happening. He slapped his pen down on the clipboard. 'Most men would cut off their right arm to be in the same room with that woman.'

The experiment wasn't working. Ralf was ordered out and taken to the washrooms. He was told to strip and stand under the shower. The water was freezing.

The female wardens entered the room and ordered Christa to remove her clothes. Pückler leaned back in his chair in the next room to watch as Christa handed back her garments one by one. She began to cry, fearing that her hopes of liberty and seeing her baby had come to nothing again. She stood by the radiator. The heat had been turned off again, and when Ralf was returned to the room some time later he was naked and shivering. His teeth were chattering, and she moved away so as to let him take the warmth.

'What the fuck do they want?' Ralf shouted at the door as soon as they locked it again.

They stood naked in front of each other, Ralf's body shaking as he began to flail his arms about him to generate circulation. Pückler allowed them time, waiting for the forces of compassion and human need to converge and bring the couple together. But Christa and Ralf remained apart, driven more by panic and the solipsistic trauma of their own fate. Nothing changed. Even the sight of each other's naked bodies did nothing to push them towards each other. Then the lights went off and the room was thrown into complete darkness.

Pückler and his guards observed Ralf and Christa on the UV screen, their green fishlike bodies still in the same position. Ralf felt his way like a blind man to one of the armchairs. Christa was curled up into a ball. They were left like this for a long time. The only thing that had changed an hour later was that Christa had got in under the blanket while Ralf remained in one of the armchairs. It seemed that even by force or by threat of death they would not submit to each other's bodies.

Then the silence was broken once more as the key spun in the lock. The lights went on again and guards rushed into the room, among them Pückler holding up a handgun. Christa had almost fallen asleep and was now told to get up, blinded by the sudden brightness. She and Ralf exchanged a desperate look under these new conditions. 'No,' Ralf shouted, but then he was immediately hit across the mouth by Pückler and told to face the wall. A guard placed a blindfold around his eyes.

There was no sound in the room except for breathing; all of these people sharing the same small pool of air. She was given her prison smock back and told to dress. The silent anxiety and the utter darkness of the previous hour were now violated by this new terror; she began to feel weak and sick. She was afraid to speak. As they escorted her out of the room again, she saw that Pückler had put his gun up to Ralf's head.

She was halfway down the corridor when a shot went off behind her, a dull clap, like the lid of a trunk slamming shut. It seemed to fill the whole prison wing with piercing echoes. The sound came from everywhere at once. Before she could utter a word or struggle to turn back towards Ralf, a guard had placed a hand over her mouth and she was dragged away.

THIRTY-SIX

Claudia ended her affair with Kevin. Now that Mathias had moved out, she began to see the Irishman in a different light, as though she couldn't bear him all of a sudden and had to find a way of extracting herself immediately. She took time off work to meet him and deliver a diplomatic speech: it was nothing personal, Kevin was a lovely man, but they had reached the end of the road. She would remain grateful to him for the way in which he had restored her spirit. He had helped her to discover that she loved her husband, Mathias. She was a new woman.

Kevin protested and maintained that he had genuinely fallen in love with her. She was being selfish and cruel. It wasn't fair to end it now; he wanted her to come and live in Ireland with him, but she smiled and shook her head. His protest then became a little undignified when he broke all the rules and complained of being used. She couldn't understand his anger and abandoned diplomacy in order to make it clear that he had absolutely no right to expect anything from her.

'And by the way, that was a really nice compliment you paid me,' she said. 'You know, what you said to Mathias. That I was a fucking ride.'

She was able to laugh about it now. But she recalled that Kevin bore a defeated expression, as though marriage and fidelity were a conspiracy against him. Claudia tried to persuade him not to take this as a blow to his manhood, and, as a concession, agreed to say goodbye in bed. Afterwards she got dressed, walked out and drove back to work, never to see him again. There were men like that at university who had inevitably left her cold: short relationships from which it was necessary to withdraw ruthlessly in order to preserve intact memories. In some cases even the breakfast conversation was too much. Along with the excitement of the past few weeks, she now felt all the terror of those brief attachments in her student days; the compromises, the loss of independence, the whole sovereignty of her life taken over and invaded by a partner. In the aftermath of the affair with Kevin, she felt a familiar release, along with a washed-out emptiness: even recalled songs on the radio which corresponded to the same sense of loss in the past; Neil Young came to mind. Her thoughts fled towards Mathias. An irrational swell of remorse, loneliness, freedom, pride, even fear of disease were all rolled into one bleak afternoon at the office until she impulsively phoned Mathias at work and said, 'I'm sorry,' nothing more.

Of course she wasn't really sorry. It was more like a signal: the only appropriate way of saying how she felt about him now. It was clumsy. She left it alone, allowing themselves time to heal the rift. It wasn't right to urge him to return home immediately, and the temporary separation would be good for them. If only she could send flowers or something.

In the following days she spent a lot of time with Werner, imposing herself a little, lying on his bed and talking to him, even trying to appreciate some of his techno-music. Werner must have thought it was weird that she should suddenly pay so much attention to him, asking him to show her how to play computer games. It was as though Werner led the way back to Mathias. And then Werner complained of being overpowered by her perfume, she was hurt but said nothing.

She felt her son wasn't reading enough and spent a ridiculous Saturday morning going through bookshops with him. Werner interpreted it correctly and asked her to phone Mathias. She spoke about the problems but didn't think it was fair to Werner to be gloomy. She was almost over-positive. Another day she bought a stack of classics for herself and felt a surge of intellectual excitement, knowing that she would now go back to more cultural pursuits. All the feckless, adolescent lust had been left behind. She even bought a new reading lamp and settled down to long evenings at home with Fontane.

She rediscovered the pleasure of walking and swimming. She felt younger. All in all, the affair had been refreshing; restoring a vital connection with the world. She allowed another week to pass by, phoning Mathias once or twice and leaving a message. Even though his absence was giving her time to readjust and face him like a new woman, she was struck by a raging curiosity; she wanted to know where he was, what he was doing. She talked to Alexandra a lot and ultimately phoned Mathias more persistently, saying they had to meet and talk. Mathias listened to her explanations but refused to meet her.

'You're punishing me, Matt,' she said in a voice that bore great dignity.

'I'm punishing you?' he retorted, but there was a sort of fatigue in his attitude towards her, as though he didn't have the time to go through this. He sounded so distant that she insisted on meeting him.

'We've nothing to talk about,' was all he would say, and it filled Claudia with such instant terror that she felt a kind of lightheaded ague, as if the office was too bright. The fear that he had actually left her for good seemed to manifest itself in a spontaneous dizziness accompanied by a tiny whirring noise in her ears.

She composed herself and left the office immediately, drove over to the *Tageszeitung* and walked right past the receptionist, scarcely saying a word. She hadn't even looked at herself in the mirror, or adjusted her hair. In less than half an hour, she had crossed Berlin and was standing there in Mathias's office staring at him, not crying, just pale and terribly serious. She folded her arms and waited for him to finish a phone call. The sight of his workplace made her feel even more distant. She noticed the sense of embarrassment with which he looked around at his colleagues before ushering her out of the office again with a kind of excessive politeness, taking her all the way down in the lift and out past the receptionist again without a single word. Outside, the noise of traffic, the fumes and the stifling heat on the pavement would have caused her to faint if Mathias hadn't quickly pulled her into a nearby Italian ice-cream parlour.

'I've found somebody,' he announced quite openly. She had already guessed that much, but hearing him say it in broad daylight made her sick with nausea. She pleaded with him, told him it was all over with Kevin; it had been a terrible mistake.

'It was just a fling, Matt. I'm different now. I don't even know why I did it. The only thing I've learned from it is that I love you, Mathias. I swear.'

'Claudia, this has got nothing to do with what you did. This is something that would have happened anyway, between myself and Christa.'

'Don't do this to us. I beg you, Mathias.'

But Mathias remained quietly obstinate. She could not understand how he could be so cold towards her. People came and went all around them. Claudia sat staring in the direction of the ice-cream counter, absently destroying her paper napkin, repeating the whole conversation over again from the start, accusing him of leaving her. But nothing changed. 'It's the Ossie girl,' she said, beginning to panic. Claudia knew she was being unsubtle; racist even. But she was suddenly consumed by jealousy which alternated with moments of sheer contempt for Mathias. 'Are the Ossie girls better in bed then?' she asked, though she instantly regretted saying it and begged him to forgive her. The tears filling her eyes again only caused more embarrassment and brought their meeting to an abrupt end.

'Claudia, we've got to go . . .' he said, and they reverted briefly to family talk: who would collect Werner and who would take him for the weekend. This was separation talk. It only made her feel marginally better that Mathias was still devoted to Werner.

Mathias continued to stay at Max Rodiger's apartment. Once

or twice he went back home to collect Werner or to get some of his clothes. Now and again he stayed with Christa in her small apartment in Pankow. They even went shopping together one Saturday morning; the true test of intimacy, wandering around the open-air market at Pankow, inspecting the cheap imitation designer labels and fake perfume.

People of all races lurked around bargain bins. One table was covered with nothing but bras, like an infinity of white pyramids. A Polish man offered three potato peelers for the price of one and tiny Vietnamese women sold cut-price cartons of cigarettes. Men sat on the park benches nearby with sunburned faces, drinking. Wasps hovered around bins and cake stalls, and everywhere in Germany that summer, women, both East and West, had turned out in their thousands wearing cycling shorts. It was the year of cycling shorts, Mathias thought, the year of luminous green thighs, the year of not looking back.

Mathias and Christa felt their lives suddenly accelerating together, leaving behind all the loose ends. Christa had by now been initiated into computer games by Werner. Mathias was still actively hunting Pückler, but they spoke less about it, as though lovers were only permitted to go forward.

Mathias was never allowed to forget about Claudia, because she kept phoning him, insisting on meeting him to discuss their marriage. She had gone into a phase of dedicated endurance. Her conversations on the phone were dignified and sad.

And then one day, out of the blue, a letter arrived from Ralf. It was addressed to Christa Süsskind, c/o *Tageszeitung*, and had apparently gone around the office for days. On the back, an address in Eisenhüttenstadt. Mathias turned the letter over and over in his hands, burning with curiosity. He phoned Christa at work. 'It's from Eisenhüttenstadt, out there on the Polish border.'

'Yes, I know where Eisenhüttenstadt is,' she said, slightly irritated. Later, when Mathias handed her the letter after work, expecting her to read it straight away, she placed it on the dashboard instead, unopened.

'Aren't you going to read it?' he said.

'Not right now, Mathias.'

Then he saw that she was crying. Tears ran steadily down her face without her uttering any sound. He put his hand on hers and some pedestrians walking in front of the car looked at him accusingly. The tears came back again in the Chinese restaurant. Wind chimes jangled constantly somewhere in the background and at a table nearby a couple were eating without a word, the woman sitting back for a breather between courses. Christa wiped her eyes with a paper napkin embossed with a red dragon. The Chinese waiter smiled and bowed continually, as though people in Germany cried over dinner out of sheer happiness.

Christa spoke very little on the way back. The sudden sight of Ralf's handwriting had become a burden to her. At Max Rodiger's apartment she placed the unopened letter on the kitchen table and took a shower. Afterwards she appeared in the living room wearing Mathias's dressing gown. She silently took the newspaper from his hands and placed a kiss on his lips. Her eyes were sad. He led her away to the bedroom. She tried not to think of Ralf, not to remember anything. The walls were bare now because she had removed the photographs of Hohenschönhausen, though the atmosphere of the prison still remained. As she lay down on the bed, Mathias closed the curtains, throwing the room into half-light, like a pale, grey-blue sunset. He stood over her for a while. He watched her untying the dressing gown and revealing her body, obeying a silent command, looking up at him and waiting. His hands were hanging by his sides, occasionally tightening into fists and letting go again. It was not until after he made love, after she began to frown, after her eyes went rolling back in ecstatic submission and the tears ran down her face, that she finally agreed to open the letter.

'Dear Christa,' she read:

It was so good to see your picture in the *Tageszeitung*. It is so good at last to know that you are alive and well. I have thought about you ever since Hohenschönhausen. I am living here in Eisenhüttenstadt, where they sent me after my release. Officially, I work as a mechanic. I served ten and a half years out of the fifteen. I tried to make contact with you on a number of occasions since then, I went back to Berlin twice. I know that a lot of time has passed now, but I want you to understand that you will always be in my mind . . .

Christa continued to read, in a trance.

. . . I am afraid I have no information about the baby. But I have been trying to trace Pückler for the past two years. I have instituted proceedings against him and against Mielke in the courts. If it takes me the rest of my life, I will get him. I know that Krombholz is now living near Frankfurt.

. . . Even though my life has now changed in various ways (I am now remarried here in Eisenhüttenstadt), I would very much like to meet you to talk about these things. But if you do not wish to, then I fully understand and wish you all the best of luck in your life –

Ralf

Christa handed the letter to Mathias and lay back silently, arms behind her head, looking up as if she were out in a field watching slow white clouds dragging across a blue sky. Mathias scanned through the letter swiftly. Frankfurt, he thought to himself. That made things very much easier.

Christa jumped out of bed and began to dress.

'Come on,' she said. 'Let's go.'

She went to the bathroom and came back wearing a pair of rose-coloured briefs. She put on a wide black skirt bearing the print of the night sky – the moon, the plough, and the firmament.

'I want to dance,' she said, spinning around, showing the flash of pink.

THIRTY-SEVEN

Claudia could not bear it any longer. It was like a breaking-point test on a piece of rope or wire cable. There was no alternative but to call on Alexandra and Klaus, to see if they could persuade Mathias not to leave his family. Alexandra was pregnant, and jubilant. They held a small celebration. The crib had already been bought and Alexandra had repainted a spare room pink. But when Claudia arrived without Mathias the evening was taken up instead by her marriage crisis. Nobody wanted to call it a separation yet.

Claudia still talked to Mathias over the phone, and they met frequently, if only briefly, on account of Werner. But the dialogue had become increasingly staccato, each conversation rotating back to the beginning again. Claudia could only repeat herself and maintain her dignity. She no longer pleaded with him, no longer apologized or asked him to forgive. The onus was on him; he was now the one who was wrecking the family. She was drinking a bit more than usual, sometimes as soon as she got home, in order to banish the loneliness. She resisted crying, resisted depression, resisted the idea of going back to Kevin. She resisted eating too much and resisted falling victim to all the allergies she once had. She discovered how much she hated television, sitting there alone allowing images to feed her emptiness. Overnight, it seemed as though every programme had begun to dwell on marriage break-up. Every song described loss.

Alexandra and Klaus went over to Max Rodiger's apartment

and talked to Mathias. Something about the sheer bliss of Alexandra's pregnancy seemed to make her the right envoy for reconciliation; they would soon be two happy families again, she predicted. She kept using the term '*Seitensprung*', or 'fling', but Mathias spoke of his new relationship with Christa as something unique and wonderful, something that could only happen once in a lifetime. Alexandra didn't put it quite so bluntly when she reported back to Claudia. Her verdict was that Mathias would soon tire of the East German woman and come round.

Claudia also communicated with Mathias through Werner, sending obscure signals through the boy's well-meaning words. Sometimes her ambassador got the messages wrong, however, bringing back signs of yielding which amounted to nothing. At other times the boy carried back only the evidence of how good a time Mathias was having: concerts, movies, restaurants. Claudia once betrayed all tact by asking him what Christa Süsskind looked like, but Werner then stopped giving any more information and settled down to a series of mute, colourless responses which showed neither hope nor despair.

It was time to confront the other woman, Claudia felt, though she kept putting it off, fearing that such a meeting would turn ugly and only alienate Mathias even further. Mathias continued to collect Werner and bring him back each time so as to give her no reason to come near Max Rodiger's apartment. But Claudia continued to formulate things to say to the East German woman, preparing for the ultimate clash. She would wipe the floor with this young Ossie girl, she vowed. Did she have any idea of the destruction she was responsible for? Did she have any shame? Did she realize that she was wrecking other people's lives? Sometimes Claudia felt more composed and relied on a dignified superiority that would allow her to meet this woman, not out of belligerence but for a bit of straight talking.

Faced with an empty weekend ahead, the meeting finally took place on a Friday evening when Claudia's despair turned to action with an early drink after work. She decided to bring

Werner over to Max Rodiger's apartment instead of waiting for Mathias. Carefully timing her arrival to avoid her husband, she found herself shaking hands politely with Christa, Werner at her side to emphasize her role as the true mother. She looked Christa up and down with mild supremacy, then more with surprise. She had not expected to see an older woman and initially restrained herself from any outburts of malice, feeling instead that she could win her over perhaps. The age difference seemed to reduce the notion of contest.

'I might as well wait for Mathias,' she said, bringing Werner into the living room. Christa gave her no encouragement and showed no hospitality. Even a smile would have been out of order. She seemed almost trapped in her role as dentist's receptionist and informed Claudia rather formally that Mathias wasn't expected back for a long while yet. Even her language was official and archaic, lacking the loose TV geniality of Western self-confidence. Werner stared out of the window at the street while the two women studied each other in furtive glances. East meets West, both of them looking their best: Christa waiting to go out to dinner dressed in a pleated red tartan skirt and a beige linen jacket with the sleeves rolled up, and Claudia wearing a more casual bottle-green silk blouse and brand new jeans, torn at one knee. Christa seemed momentarily absorbed by Claudia's black lace-up boots, and the cone-shaped chrome and leather handbag.

Claudia sat down, knowing that her silent, perhaps over-cool presence as well as her younger years gave her the edge. You could always tell East Germans, she felt; there was no way they could hide thirty years of inertia with a tartan skirt. So this is the lovers' roost, she thought to herself, looking around at the furniture and the personal effects.

Christa was still standing by the door wondering if she should go and sit down too, face up to the confrontation or simply leave Claudia on her own until Mathias arrived. She didn't want to act like a coward, nor did she want to fight, especially since

Mathias's wife was treating her with such condescension so far. Besides, Christa had nothing to feel culpable about. To break the silence she asked Werner if he'd had a good time at the kite-flying exhibition.

'Yes,' Werner responded and smiled, like a minimal indicator of the tension in the room. But the familiarity with Claudia's son finally breached the safety limit like a bi-metal snap.

'Do you not have any idea what you're doing, Fräulein . . .' Claudia finally said in a high-pitched, tearful burst of anger, shaking her head and staring incredulously at the other woman.

'I beg your pardon,' Christa said, stalling. She had no wish to enter into this confrontation.

'Do you have any idea what hurt you're causing? We're talking about a family here.'

'I don't know what you're accusing me of, Frau Hauser. Shouldn't you be talking to Mathias?'

'A person has to take responsibility for their own actions some time, that's all I have to say.' Claudia stood up, preparing to leave again. 'How would you like it if somebody came and wrecked your family?'

'Mama,' Werner intervened.

Christa could hardly believe Claudia's insensitivity. She wanted to explain her whole life to this woman but remained silent, refusing to allow herself to be drawn any further. 'You should talk to Mathias, not me.'

Claudia felt she had been extremely restrained. There was much more she could have said. She began to wander around the apartment, studying everything, even peering into the bedroom and laughing at the strip of mirror on the ceiling.

'That's really something,' she said, throwing Christa a look of acid contempt, hoping that she would fight back. But Christa refused the challenge.

'Mama, I think you'd better go,' Werner whispered.

'I don't know if you should be staying here, Werner,' Claudia contemplated. 'I don't think it's right.'

And just as she prepared to take Werner away again, Mathias arrived. Seeing Christa and Claudia together, he hesitated and went over to Werner, running his hand over the boy's head. He tried to assess how far things had gone and asked Claudia to go into the kitchen with him. Christa and Werner could hear their voices from behind the closed door. In raised tones, Claudia asked what kind of place this was to bring up a child. She mentioned the mirror on the ceiling. 'I don't think it's right, him seeing her underwear all over the place.' It wasn't the kind of environment Claudia wanted for her son. Mathias retaliated. He mentioned the used condom Werner had found at home beside Claudia's bed. And the time Werner woke up at the garden house with a nightmare and found his mother kneeling in front of the naked Irishman. The exchange got even worse and ended up in a dead-end shouting match. Then there was silence for a long time and Claudia wondered if they could ever be in love again. The breaking point had been reached.

'Come home with me,' she said. Mathias sighed and stared out through the kitchen window.

'What do you want with her?' she demanded.

'I love her,' Mathias said.

'Crap! You want to fuck her, that's all.'

'I want to help her . . . I want to find her baby. I've got to find the people who did this to her.'

Claudia laughed, mocking his chivalry. 'What, are you some kind of Stasi hunter? Some kind of new Simon Wiesenthal?'

Mathias allowed the insult to pass over him. He stared back at Claudia and suddenly began to see his own limitations.

'Be realistic, Matt . . . I'm the mother of your boy.'

In the end, he agreed to leave with Claudia. They went out into the warm evening and walked through the streets, stopping at a fountain to call a truce. It was getting dark and birds gathered noisily in the trees around the square. They could hear the U-Bahn and the traffic in the distance. She talked about good times, moments when they had been very close. She put her arms around him and proclaimed her love, but he pulled away from her and caught an expression of sadness in her eyes which he had not seen before. He couldn't bear it. He had always seen her strong side. He drove her home in her car, but the stoical silence haunted him all the way, as though for the first time he saw a delicate flaw which had remained hidden as long as they loved each other. It was something about her large round eyes. He could not look at them. He stepped out of the car and she said nothing, having no strength left to stop him except in her eyes. He walked down the street knowing that if he turned around he would see her still sitting in the car without moving.

After that, Claudia went into a hurt phase. The only solace she could find was in shopping, spending hours and hours after work buying all kinds of things she didn't even need. She had the urge to transform her home and bought things as though money didn't matter.

The shock came to Mathias when he received the credit-card statements and discovered that Claudia had gone on some kind of consumer rampage. He should have guessed something was wrong when Werner arrived back twice with various new computer accessories. Werner told him of all the new things Claudia had bought for the home. The whole apartment was full of stuff: a new TV, new washing machine, dinner plates, a service trolley, dozens of CDs; too many things for Werner to grasp. The spare room was full of items which had not even been opened: kitchen utensils, sheets; even things like stationery, books on science, natural history magazines and a set of oil paints. An easel stood in the living room with some paint splashed on a canvas, a new ghetto-blaster still in its box beside it. All over Claudia's bedroom there were clothes, new under-wear, new nightwear, everything.

Furious, Mathias went over while Claudia was at work, only to find that the apartment had been turned into a warehouse. The hopeless idiocy of her squandering had gone beyond any notion of practicality, or luxury even. It was not anger or betrayal but pure anarchy; credit-card terrorism bordering on insanity. He was frightened by her ability to achieve this in only a few days. He sat down on the sofa, only to find an unopened jewellery case containing a new man's watch. How would they bring all these things back to the stores?

'Jesus,' he said, holding he head helplessly.

His first concern was to get hold of the two Gold credit cards which were still in Claudia's possession. He spoke to her at work, cautiously, like a hostage mediator.

'Why are you doing this, Claudia? Are you trying to hurt me?'

'You don't understand, Matt. It was for you,' she said, but there was something detached and distant about her voice, as though she had gone into a dreamy dementia.

'We'll have to bring everything back,' he said.

He knew she was in trouble. They would have to meet and sort everything out. He suggested booking her in for counselling, but she mistook it for marriage counselling and was disgusted when he corrected her. He demanded the credit cards and Claudia became instantly obscene.

'Stick your card up her asshole . . .'

'Claudia, I'll meet you after work. Be there,' he shouted.

He put the phone down and went round the apartment, gathering all the new items together. There were tears in his eyes. He felt his life was finished, calculating bankruptcy. Thousands of marks worth of goods; enough napkin rings to run a hotel. Not in years had he found himself emotionally so overcome.

He phoned to cancel the credit cards, explaining that they had gone missing. He was reluctant to say stolen. Then he rang up to cancel two airline tickets to New York which Claudia had simply thrown on to the oak trunk in the hallway. It touched him that she had booked these flights, as some kind of reconciliation journey to a new place. On his way back to work it struck him that the garden house might also contain something new, so he drove straight out there and found the place stuffed with new gardening tools, a grass machine and a hedge trimmer. There was too much even to take with him, so he merely locked the door again and left. He beat his fist on the roof of the car.

THIRTY-EIGHT

On the way to Eisenhüttenstadt, Christa was in a strange, elated mood at first. She played around with the tape deck, adjusted her seat, foraged in the glove compartment and found a pair of sunglasses which belonged to Claudia. Hiding all her concern about the situation with Mathias, she threw off her shoes and placed her bare feet on the dashboard, listening to the music. This was the only way to travel back into the former GDR, she thought, in a BMW, with her feet up and her arm around Mathias.

Many of the roads had already been paved over by the unified state, but here and there she could still feel the cracks and potholes of the old Soviet roads. It felt like driving back into a black and white film, as though some mental filter extracted all the colour from the landscape; it had been wiped clean by successive waves of shifting history. The car removed her from reality.

Mathias had been to this flat and unforgiving hinterland around the Oder/Neisse line before. It was no wonder that former prisoners like Ralf Krone had been banished here after their release, he thought. Everywhere, the system had left its mark – the pollution, the decay, the high-rise suburbs on the edge of each town.

Christa took her feet down long before Eisenhüttenstadt. She gathered herself together and stared out at the giant steelworks looming silent and empty in the distance like an abandoned, rusting fairground. Only a handful of men still worked there.

Perfect sugarloaf hills of gravel had begun to sprout short grass. Thistles and ragweed proliferated through cracked concrete. Nothing had ever decayed so fast – trolleys, cranes, conveyor belts. Metal doors banged in the breeze, and the stationary bucket elevators were full of stagnant water from the last rain.

The town itself was more picturesque, though colourless too: a fortress of picket fences; a small market square surrounded by shabby medieval remains on the Oder river. Its name had been changed back to the original Fürstenberg/Oder. They found the house on the main street where Ralf lived. Ralf's wife answered the door and explained that he was in the allotment on the outskirts of the town.

'You must be Christa,' she said. 'I'm so glad to meet you.' They shook hands and Ralf's wife directed them to the allotment, down the road and right towards the river.

Mathias and Christa walked to where they could see a patchwork of gardens with ripening fruit trees – apple, pear, cherry, plum. Some of the allotments had wooden shacks, some were surrounded by rose-clad rustic fences. Beyond them the river flowed swiftly and silently, birds occasionally dipping down over the surface of the green-brown water. They found Ralf standing at the centre of an apiary with bees flying about everywhere in the afternoon sunshine. Seeing him there in front of her, back from the dead almost, she was hit by a peculiar set of emotions; fear, sadness, joy; she could not tell which. He was working without any protection and the air around him was a constellation of black dots and vectors, bees on his face and on his back, like tiny dangerous pets clinging to their owner.

'Christa,' Ralf said, when he spotted her. He stepped towards her with his arms out but the bees prevented him from going any closer. Christa took a step backwards.

'Just one moment,' he said moving away to the other end of the garden until the bees abandoned him and returned to their hives.

They walked back into the town together. Ralf looked well,

suntanned and healthy. At the house his wife, Gudrun, asked everyone to sit down under a sun canopy, pulling out deck chairs. Ralf and Christa remained standing for a moment, looking at each other in silence while his wife withdrew inside to make the coffee. Tears finally overwhelmed Christa as Ralf embraced her. She seemed more like a prodigal daughter than a lost lover.

'You've no idea how happy I am to see you, Christa,' he said.

'I thought you were dead . . .' she said.

'Yes, I thought the same about you for a while, but then I knew it was Pückler's trick.'

Ralf stood there holding both of her hands, like a faded incarnation from the past. Gudrun came out with the coffee and they sat down.

'I heard the shot in the cell,' Ralf continued. 'But after a few weeks, I began to think about it. Why would he have killed you and kept me alive? If anything he wanted me dead.'

Mathias complimented Ralf's wife on her damson tart. A wasp began to hover around the table. Ralf kept talking, often halting his fork on the way to his mouth, then putting it down again the way Christa remembered. He and Christa spent a long time discussing everything that happened, communicating in an arcane code of facts.

'I wrote a book while I was in prison,' he told them.

'Really? Have you still got it?' Christa asked.

'No. It was taken away from me.' Ralf explained how he had managed to write 400 pages about the abduction and the trial. The book had kept him alive for ten and a half years until the day of his release, when Pückler told him it needed a new ending.

'He shredded it.'

But Ralf told Christa he would have the last laugh. He had now begun to write the book again.

'Since I talked to you on the phone, I started writing. I've bought the paper. I'm already on page twenty.'

Ralf stood up and went into the house. He came back minutes

178

later, not with the manuscript, but with a bottle of Schnapps.

'We must drink to survival,' he announced, pouring the freezing liquid into glass tumblers and raising a toast. It was as though hundreds of small gatherings all over Eastern Europe were going through the same ritual that afternoon, over and over again toasting the death of communism.

'We met some swine in our time, you and I,' he said to Christa. 'If I ever get my hands on Pückler . . .'

'Ralf,' Gudrun said. 'Don't let yourself get bitter.'

Mathias asked how he knew that Krombholz was in Frankfurt, and Ralf began to explain how he had recently gone home to Erfurt to visit his parents' grave.

'Rainer's mother still lives there. The postman is a friend of mine and he told me that old Frau Krombholz receives a monthly cheque in the post from Frankfurt/Main.'

Years of postal interception in the GDR had become a force of habit. Ralf had even been able to find out the address and the bank account which Krombholz's firm used. But Ralf was not interested in going there to seek justice.

'Don't you think Krombholz should be prosecuted?' Mathias said.

'Not for me,' Ralf said. He seemed to have transcended the need for this reckoning. He looked older, happier and more serene than ever before, Christa thought. 'I have my book now. I have the power to rewrite everything. I don't need the satisfaction of justice.'

Christa told Ralf of their discovery, that Mareille Krombholz had taken her baby. The revelation silenced Ralf and made him think for a while. 'The baby . . .'

'It's a boy,' Christa said.

'I don't know what to hope for him. I suppose you want him back? What age would he be now, fourteen? A young Krombholz . . . or Breitkreutz, that's the name they now call themselves.'

He wrote out the address of a security firm. Perhaps Krombholz should be charged. But what about the baby? Ralf seemed confused by these new facts. Christa stayed for a long time, and they began talking about more recent things and how time had moved on. It was difficult to leave. Ralf promised to visit them in Berlin soon, and when Mathias and Christa eventually made it into the street Ralf suddenly remembered something and ran back inside. He came out again holding a brown envelope which he handed to Christa.

The BMW was parked across the mosaic pavement. Over those few hours the town seemed to have remained static, except for the few inhabitants who had skirted around the car, speculating about the afternoon visitors. A cat darted out from underneath. Ralf and his wife stood in the street until they were out of sight.

On the drive back to Berlin, Christa opened the envelope and found a cassette which she examined for a while without a word. She could have played it on the car stereo, but placed it back in the envelope and put it on the floor by her feet.

She wasn't ready to talk about it, or play it to Mathias, or even to herself. Mathias spoke about going to Frankfurt to find Krombholz, and her son. But she wasn't ready for that either and remained silent for most of the journey, absorbed by memory. Some time later she reached down and took the cassette out again. This time it appeared as though she was going to play it, but instead she attempted to break it open, smashing it against the dashboard as though that were the only way of knowing what was inside. She then took a nail file out of her bag and finally managed to prize the cassette open, liberating yards and yards of thin brown ribbon all over her lap. Mathias could only observe in silence as she opened the window and released the tape, bit by bit, to the wind, until it eventually snapped and flew clear in a swirling brown cloud, leaving the empty shell behind in her hand. She looked at the name Blondi and the number written in tiny handwriting on the label, then threw it out as well, where it clattered on the Autobahn and was soon run over and smashed for good by the unending stream of cars and trucks going in the direction of Berlin. The mass of crinkled brown tape came to rest where it snagged on the bushes of the island between the lanes of traffic, continuing to flutter and hiss and lie down, and rise up again, violently blown about by each passing windstream.

THIRTY-NINE

On a humid afternoon, three days later, Mathias drove up outside a security firm in Rüsselsheim named Fest Gmbh. It had taken some persuasion to get Christa to go through with this. Having followed her child's imaginary progress each year through the random presence of other children in shops or on the way home from school, she was eager, but also afraid of approaching that moment where her son would leap into real life. They had driven through the industrial district of Frankfurt, past Opel car manufacturers, past factories with their neatly kept patches of green shrubbery out front, arriving in a street of warehouses, garages and small processing firms. Fest Securities was on the first floor. There was a dark green Mercedes parked outside and the sound of barking in a compound at the rear.

Christa caught sight of the savage dogs through a gap in the gates and it surprised her that she felt no fear, as though she didn't possess the energy to be afraid any more. They waited on the other side of the street, watching people lock up and go home. The longer it went on, the more uncomfortable it was to be cast in the role of pursuit. Then a woman emerged from the building, followed some time later by a man.

'My God,' Christa said, sitting forward. 'It's Rainer. Look how heavy he's become.'

She shrank back in her seat again, as if she'd been spotted herself, but the obese and bald Krombholz got into the Mercedes without seeing them. Mathias followed the car at a distance, allowing the Mercedes to pull out of sight around the corner each time, before racing along to the next junction. They hadn't gone very far before Krombholz pulled up outside a well-kept apartment block; a sprinkler hose sent a continuous figure of eight of water across the lawn.

Mathias had all but given up hope of ever find Pückler. The sight of Krombholz stepping out of the car, locking the doors behind him with a tiny electronic yelp and walking towards the building carrying a briefcase, now consumed all their attention. Christa had not spoken much, funnelling all her anger and bitterness into this moment of supreme patience. Mathias jumped out of the car first, followed by Christa. Just as Krombholz reached the entrance to the apartment block, Mathias called out his name and Krombholz stopped. It took a moment before he turned around and held out his hand in a gesture of incomprehension.

'There must be some mistake,' he smiled, but then he recognized Christa and looked about nervously.

'There is no mistake, Rainer.'

'Christa . . .'

Krombholz immediately tried to negotiate with her. He began to panic and make sure that he wasn't being observed; conscious of scandal, hoping that Christa and Mathias would just go away again. Amazed that this moment of reckoning had finally come, he offered her money, lots of money, as though unable to understand the concept of remorse, or justice; only commerce. Sweat broke out over his large face, turning years of internalized guilt and fear into instant cowardice. His sense of humour had deserted him long ago.

'Christa,' he appealed, breathing heavily and coming towards her with his arms out as a friend.

'Stay away from me,' she said firmly, holding up her hand.

Krombholz backed off again, stepping out of the sunlight and loosening his tie against the stickiness of the afternoon. He seemed breathless. Christa watched as though the sheer satisfaction of examining his nervous behaviour was enough. The water hose continued to hiss and spit. Other people came and went through the doorway, increasing his discomfort, pinning him back in a silent prosecution until he was forced to ask Christa and Mathias to come in. They went up in the lift together; without a word, perspiring, like the moment before a trial.

The apartment on the fourth floor carried the name of Breitkreutz. Mareille came to the door as they entered, standing back with a smile crumbling away on her face, apron straps undone, the smell of roast pork in the background. The television was on without any sound.

'My God, Christa,' she said, holding her trembling hands up to her mouth, barely able to pronounce her name without a sigh of despair. Christa remained unmoved.

'What could we do, Christa?' Krombholz began, once they had gone inside. 'We had to look after your baby. It was the only thing left to us, isn't that so, Mareille?'

'You betrayed us,' Christa said. 'You organized the abduction. You set us up. My baby was your reward, isn't that so?'

'No,' Krombholz said. He had taken out a handkerchief and began mopping his forehead. 'It wasn't like that. They were different times, Christa.'

'We had to look after your baby,' Mareille assisted. 'We had every intention of giving him back, but then we couldn't . . .'

'It was Pückler. We were not allowed.'

Christa looked at Mathias. She could not accept any of this. The smell of roast pork enveloped the scene in a cloud of heavy cosiness. What a strange combination of hospitality and terror, she thought. The personal effects around the living room of the apartment pointed to a familiar but impenetrable family life: curtains, pictures, blue upholstered sofas, plants and hi-fi; an ordinary combination of tastes and idiosyncrasies which conspired to alienate the intruder. It seemed odd that the same images should come up on the TV here as elsewhere. It seemed odd that nobody was watching. Everyone remained standing, as though it would be outrageous to sit down and discuss things rationally.

'Where is my son?' Christa demanded.

'You can't take the child away from us,' Mareille implored, tearing absently at her apron. Krombholz tried to offer money again.

'Don't be too hard on us. We can give you money, Christa. Just say what you want, we'll make it up to you. Name a figure.'

'Where is the boy?' Christa repeated more forcefully, showing nothing but contempt for his money. She could see a framed photograph of Rainer and Mareille with the boy in bathing trunks on the bookcase.

'Don't destroy his life,' Mareille said in a low voice; an appeal from one mother to another. 'Peter doesn't know anything about this. It's not fair to him if you change everything now . . .

'He'll be back any minute,' she continued, glancing at the clock. 'He's at his piano lesson.'

Peter, Christa thought. The name of the boy filled her with great excitement, as though she had known it all the time. She saw the piano in the corner and thought of Ralf's musical talent. She began to take in other intimate possessions around the room, like the knick-knacks and holiday trophies; a screwdriver and a pair of scissors standing in a silver tankard. She wondered where her son slept at night.

Krombholz turned his back on them and began to stare out through the window at other apartment blocks and at the mosaic of red roofs and green patches of grass and trees stretching below him into the distance. He leaned his fists on the window sill, allowing his weight to fall on them, knuckles turning white with the pressure. His head sank down as though the view over this suburb had turned sour, drained of all radiance, reducing his success and happiness to nothing. He could find no words to express the sudden emptiness out there. His shoulders began to shake and Christa could hear the first halting, almost inaudible notes of his sobbing. His fists shifted outwards along the marble sill under his weight, slowly dislodging a potted plant until it was pushed to the edge. It tipped over and fell to the floor in slow motion with a cushioned thud. Nobody seemed able to stop it from crashing down, scattering the peaty soil over the carpet. He was unaware of it himself. He kept on sinking down and down with each heaving sob until his head lay pressed against the glass.

'Rainer,' Mareille exclaimed. She gathered her senses and went over to pick up the plant and put it further back on the window sill. She placed a broken shard beside it and checked that the plant was all right.

'Rainer, come on. Don't let Peter see you like this.' She attempted to scoop up the loose clay with her hands, then went into the kitchen to fetch a dustpan and brush, muttering as she began to sweep up the mess.

The door opened. In the entrance to the apartment stood a chubby fourteen-year-old boy with short, spiky blond hair. He was biting into a Snickers bar. He pulled it out of his mouth at the sight of strangers in the living room. He stood there in his trainers and shiny anorak. Emblazoned across his moss-green T-shirt was the word 'MOTORHEAD', in fiery gothic lettering. His face was spattered with random spots. His mouth hung open.

FORTY

The summer had almost come to an end. School was about to
start again and Claudia brought Werner into the city for a treat.
She wanted to buy him some new clothes and a new schoolbag,
very reasonable things which the boy needed badly. All the
goods from her big shopping spree had been returned. It had
taken a whole day for Mathias to deliver everything back again,
coming and going with packages and boxes while she sat in the
kitchen drinking gin and tonics, occasionally identifying the
origins of a particular item or pointing out something which was
not new, like the vacuum cleaner. She had been less desolate that
afternoon while Mathias was there, moving around the rooms –
if not back with the family, then at least demonstrating involuntarily that he was still committed in some way.

Claudia had become more calm. The rage of that shopping
hysteria made way for a more clearheaded campaign of talking
with Mathias. She was eating more and drinking more, but
perhaps she now understood the elemental properties of time
more clearly, as though she had learned unlimited patience.
With school starting, life would soon return to some normality.

Werner and Claudia spent a long time going around the
shops in Taunzienstrasse together. After an hour trawling
through comic shops, record stores and computer stores, they
moved on to clothes, and Werner eventually decided on an
American NFL jacket with the Buffalo markings. He no longer
wanted to wear dinosaur underwear. His T-shirts had to be
Beavis and Butthead. There was only one brand of shoes he

could wear; nothing else would do, even if it took almost an hour to find them.

They stopped for a cake and a chocolate drink. Werner took the opportunity to put on his new jacket. He wore a baseball cap the wrong way round and Claudia could not help laughing every time she looked at him. As they walked along through the shops again, he seemed to have discovered a new way of walking: a bouncing saunter attached itself to his step as though he had suddenly gained infinite self-confidence. He looked cool and indestructible. Even with all the shopping bags in her hand, Claudia could not help laughing and imitating the new spring in his gait, stopping at the top of the escalator in Ka De We to control herself again.

Later on, when they could carry no more bags, they went for something to eat. Werner insisted on McDonald's; it was his choice, since he was going back to school; a Hauser tradition.

Claudia felt exposed in the brightly lit fast-food hall. She felt the lighting was designed to make people look ugly, or hungry. They sat at a table in the upstairs eating area amid the constant flow of people entering and leaving. Staff in uniform and green baseball caps, turned the right way round, kept hovering over tables to take away the next empty tray, watching for signs on people's faces that they were finished.

Werner had only begun his hamburger when he wanted to go to the lavatory. He remembered his new walk along the way. Claudia watched him, smiling, her elbows on the table and the hamburger raised up to the level of her mouth like a mechanical crane. She was aware that her legs were wide apart, clamping all the shopping bags between them, and moved everything around so that she could sit more comfortably, pinning the bags against the single steel bole of the table underneath.

As soon as Werner got into the washroom he noticed a group of older boys hunched together, scuffling. He stood inside the door for a moment and heard them laughing. There was somebody sitting on the floor, being held down, and somebody else pissing into his face. Before Werner could react at all, the group broke up and turned towards him in a sudden frenzy, running past, back into the dining area one by one. One boy punched Werner in the face; another one brought his boot up swiftly to meet his groin, almost as an integral athletic feature of his running motion. Werner bent over obediently for the pain, but he could not avoid looking up at the yelping, jumping procession of boys, as though seeing were a form of protection. Some of them were shavenheaded, some dressed in jackets bearing symbols which he could not identify in that short space of time. One of them wore a Bavarian hat and seemed to look at him in passing with the glazed and satisfied expression of a puppet. Laughing with contrived mirth, they filed away towards the exit, leaving a man sitting on the floor behind them with his head against the urinal; mouth open, face wet and glistening, spitting convulsively to rid himself of the foul taste in his mouth. He held a darker stain of blood around his chest with his hand. One of the assailants ran out zipping up his trousers, howling a short, exotic war cry which echoed through the cubicles, while the last of them, triumphantly holding a wallet in one hand and a knife in the other, followed, casually slashing the knife at Werner and striking him on the shoulder, just at the base of the neck. Werner felt the point of the weapon entering his shoulder like a giant bee-sting and sank down, feeling the warm faucet of blood in his hand. He became dizzy and slumped over with his head on the floor in such a manner that he could now see the door finally closing sideways, leaving an abrupt silence behind in the wash-rooms.

Claudia heard them coming out, barking and running; dancing almost through the aisle, some of them laughing as they knocked over milkshakes and threw french fries into the air. Somebody had already shouted for the police. Another woman shook her head. An obese and red-faced man looking straight at Claudia simply said, 'Idioten.'

There followed a moment when everything began to return to

normal; somebody asked to be compensated for the spoiled food. But then came a further commotion from the washrooms and people began to rush away from the tables around her. When Werner had not come back, she began to join the apprehension and stood up to see, not quite wanting to leave the shopping bags behind. It was only when she heard people calling for an ambulance that she was hit by a sense of panic and rushed through the onlookers standing around the door of the washrooms. A man was kneeling down over Werner, pinching Werner's shoulder tight, making it look as though he was draining all the colour from the boy's face. His eyes were open in a blank stare. There was blood all over Werner's new jacket. She called out his name in a sort of hoarse, inaudible scream, fell on her knees and held his head until the ambulance men came.

Where are you now, Mathias, she kept saying to herself, perhaps even out loud. In the ambulance, she was unaware of anything but talking to Mathias, begging him to come, asking him why he wasn't with them. Even on the phone at the hospital she didn't quite perceive it as part of reality until she heard him speaking. She couldn't cry. She could only report everything chronologically in a detached and even tone.

'Claudia, I'm coming immediately,' he said, and she was left holding the phone in the corridor outside Intensive Care as though she had been struck dumb. What kept her from collapsing was the deeply embedded instinct of motherhood and the fact that she felt responsible for everything. The scent of disinfectant seemed to make her numb. She felt cold in her summer clothes. Nurses offered her a sedative but Claudia wanted to remain fully aware until she heard what was happening to Werner. She was even aware of trivialities like the shopping bags left behind in McDonald's. But then the female surgeon came out from the operating theatre to speak to her with an expression that first seemed terribly dispassionate, but soon yielded into a minimal smile: '. . . you have one hell of a lucky boy there,' she said. It seemed like an arbitrary verdict, at the toss of a coin, bringing sudden luck instead of sudden disaster. Werner had lost a lot of blood but they had missed a crucial artery. The other victim had not been so fortunate.

By the time Mathias arrived, Werner had been moved out of Intensive Care into a private room where he slept, Claudia sitting beside him in a reverie of relief. She could have collapsed or fainted now, watching Werner's serene breathing and the colour beginning to come back to his face, but she stayed alert and fully conscious, trying not to think back to the events in the restaurant.

She stood up when Mathias arrived. He walked straight towards her and took her into his arms, holding on for a long time, saying nothing. It seemed like five minutes at least before he stood back with tears in his eyes. He would not let her speak about what had happened. He just sat down with her, holding Werner's hand and hers, kissing one or the other alternately in a slow recurring relay, staring with such fervour into Claudia's eyes that he seemed to be saying he would never leave again.

FORTY-ONE

It was not until over a week later, after Werner was brought
home from the hospital, that Mathias met Christa. She understood the difficulties. They had discussed lots of things over the
phone: Krombholz, Claudia, Werner; but they agreed to post-
pone any explanations for fear of speaking out of emotion rather
than reason. They needed a really good talk.

When he finally drove out to her apartment in Pankow, she
had made up her mind about everything. It was all clear; of
course he had to go back and live with his wife and his son again.
There was no question in her mind about it, and a new
expression of contentment began to add to her resolve. He was
initially puzzled, offended even, by her suggestions, as though
she were trying to get rid of him, back to his wife.

'Why?' he asked. He had never had his mind made up for him
before and was ready to rebut everything.

'I think it's only right that you should go back to her,' she
insisted. 'You're a family. And Werner is such a lovely boy. You
have an obligation to them, and you love them. I couldn't take
part in breaking up a family.'

Mathias resisted and shook his head. But she silenced him and
continued to unfold her decision, sitting him down on the bed
where they had lain together many times. She was saying what
he wished to say himself but couldn't.

'I thought we wanted to be together,' he said uncomfortably,
almost as a retreating declaration of love which was no longer
valid.

'I want to ask you a favour, Mathias,' she said, looking him in the eyes. '. . . I don't know how you feel about this. I know you might not want agree to do it, but I would really like to have a baby. I've had one child taken from me, so I want this one to be mine alone. Nothing would make me happier.'

He didn't know what to say without offending her. His eyes turned away and scanned the room of her small, neatly kept apartment, looking for new meaning. He had only just had the life of his own son miraculously given back to him. And he had spent months trying to find Christa's son. He tried to conceal his surprise, but he was blinded by all the complications simultaneously springing to mind. Caught between the rational nature of his profession and the strength of his feelings, he thought of having to be a father, of having to support this child, of explaining everything to Claudia.

'Christa, let's not make any decisions like that now,' he said, holding her hand, looking around again as though the objects in her room could give him some inspiration. 'Let's think this out clearly.'

'But I have thought about it,' she said. 'I really want a baby. Time is running out for me.'

'Christa, wait. I'm just not sure that I can take this on right now. What would I tell Claudia?'

'Mathias, I'm not asking you to become involved. I wouldn't be a burden to you.'

She had worked everything out. It was like a lucid vision into infinity, a world starting all over again from this day onwards. It had given her a great sense of independence, a clear-headed self-assurance which would be impossible to dislodge. This would give her total independence. It would liberate her from the past, from everyone.

'What about Peter?' he asked, but she had already begun to work on that too. It would all be done on the basis of reconciliation. Nothing could have been achieved by justice or vengeance. In order to see her son, she had to introduce herself to

Peter initially as a former friend of the family going back to the GDR days. She had been back in touch with Mareille and Rainer. She would put everything behind her and make friends with them. Peter would come to Berlin from time to time, and in due course the Krombholzes would tell him everything. But it was too late to change anything back. A new beginning would give her the power to take control of her own life at last. It could not be expected to erase what had taken place before. Instead, it would bring a kind of retrospective justice and hope which would make it possible to live with the past.

'I wouldn't ask you to provide for us. I wouldn't need a penny, Mathias, honestly. And I'm not asking you to be a father.'

'But I would have to, Christa.'

'No, I insist, Mathias. I'm not asking you to get involved. I would bring this child up on my own. It would be lovely, of course, if you could be with us sometimes. It would be lovely for the child to know its father. But that would be up to you.'

'Christa?' He was still not sure. He recalled the time Claudia asked if they should have a baby, how eagerly he had said yes. But Christa's request was so strange, so insular. She was asking him to conceive a child, the very thing that would make him superfluous and give her total freedom.

'You could come and visit us,' she assured him. 'Whenever you wanted to. And if you want to tell Claudia, that's fine. But she mustn't think that I would come between you.'

'Maybe it would be better if she didn't know,' he said, not realizing that he had half consented.

They sat in silence for a moment, watching a thin beam of sunlight cutting through the room, drawing a bright, elongated diamond on the floor and illuminating a million dancing particles of dust. The window was open an inch or two and every time somebody opened a door, far away in another part of the building, the particles of dust went wild and the curtain behind them would billow as though it were inhaling a deep breath. Voices drifted up too, and faded again. Then a door would bang

194

shut somewhere. She examined his eyes as though this far-away sound had somehow made up his mind.

For a long time they sat there, absorbing this new trajectory into the future. After a while they could only repeat themselves in a kind of mindless state of suspended reality, talking until their thoughts had spun out of control and reached a spectacular momentum, like the thousands of dust particles in the room. The shape on the floor became longer and less pronounced. Soon it would be 4 p.m.; Christa could tell it almost like a clock. The stillness began to descend on the room again in dreamy layers of heat. Christa took off her shoes and lay back on the bed, patting the bedcover beside her with her hand.

FORTY-TWO

Claudia and Werner were in the water. It was the last warm weekend of the summer. School had already started. Claudia could see the bright scar at the base of Werner's neck until he swam around and clung to her from behind, hanging in the water with his arms around her waist. Then for a while she made a stirrup out of her joined hands so that he could stand up out of the water and somersault.

Neither of them saw the rain coming. A thick, deep blue summer cloud had crept up from the shore, where the swimmers could see nothing until it began to block the sun. Before Werner and his mother got out of the water it began to rain heavily in big cool drops, bouncing on the surface of the lake. The people on the shore were already running away, holding up towels and newspapers. Even though Claudia and Werner were wet from the lake, the rain seemed to add to it. Their towels and shoes were soaked, and as they ran along the sandy path up to the allotment the rain suddenly intensified into a furious shower, raising the strong smell of dampened dust and sand up into the air.

Claudia held her shoes up over her head, just to keep the big drops out of her eyes. Werner had to guide her. Their bare feet were muddy and the mud squished up between their toes. Werner laughed and whooped along with the steady drumming of the rain on roof tiles, on tables, deck chairs, flagstones and on the broad leaves of rhubarb and pumpkin and courgettes. As they reached the garden house, Claudia ran around to bring all the chair covers in, but it was already too late. Two of Werner's comics lay on the table in a soggy mass of colour. A bee lay struggling on its back, hit by the rain. They stood under the canopy waiting for the cloud to pass over.

Mathias was expected back any minute with the shopping. As he drove slowly along the lane towards the allotment, the tyres of his car merged with the steady sound of the rain so that nobody heard him. The engine made no noise either and the downpour eclipsed his arrival altogether, except perhaps for the subconscious sound of the handbrake, like a tiny, distant cracking of knuckles. Claudia knew that she would only have to look out and see him.

But the sheer weight of the rain kept Mathias in the car and prevented him from going inside. The large drops kept bouncing off the bonnet. He switched off the windscreen wipers and soon he could see nothing but the vague, watery outline of the trees and lake beyond; it was like sitting in a car wash. For an instant he knew what it would be like to have driven on that bit further, straight into the lake. He had often imagined it. He became impatient, as though he had really done it this time and the water was slowly seeping into the car. He would have to break out and swim to the surface.

He wanted to run to the garden house, to be sitting down inside with Claudia and Werner, but the water had overpowered him, holding him still, a hostage in his car until he perceived a change over the lake and knew by the faint blue brightness at the top of the windscreen that the cloud was passing. The rain eased. The drumming ceased and turned into a gurgling. By the time Claudia heard him slam the door of the car, by the time she looked out to see him pushing the gate with his back, holding the box of groceries in his arms, the sun was already out, lifting the steam up from the path and the lawn and the mushy comics.